"Am I A Hostage?"

Caroline stared at Karim while a million unnamed dreams shattered into dust.

"It is natural that you will feel anger."

"Why do they say you are a prince? Are you?" Her voice seemed to be coming from a distance.

"Caroline, come upstairs where we can talk in comfort," he urged her. "There is much to tell you, much for you to understand."

"If I have a choice, it is to leave this place now. If I have no choice, I await Your Majesty's order. But I will not pretend that I go anywhere willingly in your company."

"Then I order you upstairs," he replied calmly.

Without a word she turned and preceded him through the arched entry that only a few hours ago had seemed like the doorway to magic to her....

go through. She had tried and failed to call David earlier, then had given up, showered and dressed. She was wearing

Dear Reader,

April brings showers, and this month Silhouette Desire wants to shower you with six new, passionate love stories!

Cait London's popular Blaylock family returns in our April MAN OF THE MONTH title, *Blaylock's Bride*. Honorable Roman Blaylock grapples with a secret that puts him in a conflict between confiding in the woman he loves and fulfilling a last wish.

The provocative series FORTUNE'S CHILDREN: THE BRIDES continues with Leanne Banks's *The Secretary and the Millionaire*, when a wealthy CEO turns to his assistant for help in caring for his little girl.

Beverly Barton's next tale in her 3 BABIES FOR 3 BROTHERS miniseries, *His Woman, His Child*, shows a rugged heartbreaker transformed by the heroine's pregnancy. Powerful sheikhs abound in *Sheikh's Ransom*, the Desire debut title of Alexandra Sellers's dramatic new series, SONS OF THE DESERT. A marine gets a second chance at love in *Colonel Daddy*, continuing Maureen Child's popular series BACHELOR BATTALION. And in Christy Lockhart's *Let's Have a Baby!*, our BACHELORS AND BABIES selection, the hero must dissuade the heroine from going to a sperm bank and convince her to let *him* father her child—the old-fashioned way!

Allow Silhouette Desire to give you the ultimate indulgence— all six of these fabulous April romance books!

Enjoy!

Joan Marlow Golan
Senior Editor, Silhouette Desire

Please address questions and book requests to:
Silhouette Reader Service
U.S.: 3010 Walden Ave., P.O. Box 1325, Buffalo, NY 14269
Canadian: P.O. Box 609, Fort Erie, Ont. L2A 5X3

SHEIKH'S RANSOM
ALEXANDRA SELLERS

SILHOUETTE *Desire*

Published by Silhouette Books

America's Publisher of Contemporary Romance

For Lilia
who looks just like a Greek statue, and
who understood because her mother is an artist

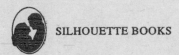 SILHOUETTE BOOKS

ISBN 0-373-76210-0

SHEIKH'S RANSOM

Printed in U.S.A.

ALEXANDRA SELLERS

was born in Ontario, and raised in Ontario and Saskatchewan. She first came to London to attend the Royal Academy of Dramatic Art and fell in love with the city. Later, she returned to make it her permanent home. Now married to an Englishman, she lives near Hampstead Heath. As well as writing romance, she teaches a course called "How To Write a Romance Novel" in London several times a year.

Because of a much-regretted allergy, she can have no resident cat, but she receives regular charitable visits from three cats who are neighbors.

Readers can write to her at P.O. Box 9449, London, NW3 2WH, England.

THE BARAKAT EMIRATES

KINGDOM OF PARVAN

Mountains of Noor

Rafi's Capital

Lake Parvaneh

Jalal's Stronghold

Iskandiyar (Ancient Site)

CENTRAL BARAKAT

River al Sa'adat

Omar's Capital

EAST BARAKAT

GULF OF BARAKAT

River al Sa'adat

WEST BARAKAT

Barakat al Barakat (Emirates Capital)

Karim's Capital

SHEIKH'S RANSOM, *Prince Karim's story*, April 1999
THE SOLITARY SHEIKH, *Prince Omar's story*, May 1999
BELOVED SHEIKH, *Prince Rafi's story*, June 1999

Available only from Silhouette Desire.

Karim's Inheritance
The Jewel Seal of Shakur

There was once a king of ancient and noble lineage who ruled over a land that had been blessed by God. This land, Barakat, lying on the route of one of the old Silk Roads, had for centuries received the cultural influences of many different worlds. Its geography, too, was diverse: it bordered the sea; then the desert, sometimes bleak with its ancient ruins, sometimes golden and studded with oases, stretched inland for many miles, before meeting the foothills of snow-capped mountains that captured the rain clouds and forced them to deliver their burden in the rich valleys. It was a land of magic and plenty and a rich and diverse heritage.

But it was also a land of tribal rivalries and not infrequent skirmishes. Because the king had the ancient blood of the Quraishi kings in his veins, no one challenged his right to the throne, but many of the tribal chieftains whom he ruled were in constant jealousy over their lands and rights against the others.

One day, the king of this land fell in love with a foreign woman. Promising her that he would never take another wife, he married her and made her his queen. This beloved wife gave him two handsome sons. The king loved them as his own right hand. Crown Prince Zaid and his brother were all that he could wish for in his sons—handsome, noble, brave warriors, and popular with his people. As they attained the age of majority, the sheikh could look forward to his own death without fear for his country, for if anything should happen to the Crown Prince, his brother Aziz would step into his shoes and be equally popular with the people and equally strong among the tribes.

Then one day, tragedy struck the sheikh and his wife. Both their sons were killed in the same accident. Now his own death became the great enemy to the old man, for with it, he knew, would come certain civil war as the tribal chieftains vied for supremacy.

His beloved wife understood all his fears, but she was by now too old to hope to give him another heir. One day, when all the rituals of mourning were complete, the queen said to her husband, "According to the law, you are entitled to four wives. Take, therefore, my husband, three new wives, that God may bless one of them with a son to inherit your throne."

The sheikh thanked her for releasing him from his promise. A few weeks later, on the same day so that none should afterwards claim supremacy, the sheikh married three beautiful young women, and that night, virile even in his old age, he visited each wife in turn, no one save himself knowing in which order he visited them. To each wife he promised that if she gave him a son, her son would inherit the throne of Barakat.

The sheikh was more virile than he knew. Each of his new wives conceived, and gave birth, nine months later, to a lusty son. And each was jealous for her own son's inheritance. From that moment the sheikh's life became a burden to him, for each of his new young wives had different reasons for believing that her own son should be named the rightful heir to the throne.

The Princess Goldar, whose exotically hooded green eyes she had bequeathed to her son, Omar, based her claim on the fact that she herself was a descendant of the ancient royal family of her own homeland, Parvan.

The Princess Nargis, mother of Rafi and descended from the old Mughal emperors of India, had in addition given birth two days before the other two wives, thus making her son the firstborn.

The Princess Noor, mother of Karim, claimed the inheritance for her son by right of blood—she alone of the wives was an Arab of noble descent, like the sheikh himself. Who but her son to rule the desert tribesmen?

The sheikh hoped that his sons would solve his dilemma for him, that one would prove more princely than the others. But as they grew to manhood, he saw that each of them was, in his own way, worthy of the throne, that each had the nobility the people would look for in their king, and talents that would benefit the kingdom were he to rule.

When his sons were eighteen years old, the sheikh knew that he was facing death. As he lay dying, he saw each of his young wives in turn. To each of them again he promised that her son would inherit. Then he saw his three sons together, and on them he laid his last command. Then, last of all, he saw the wife and companion of his life, with whom he had seen such happiness and such sorrow. To her willing care he committed his young wives and their sons, with the assistance of his vizier Nizam al Mulk, whom he appointed Regent jointly with her.

When he died the old sheikh's will was revealed: the kingdom was to be divided into three principalities. Each of his sons inherited one principality and its palace. In addition, they each inherited one of the ancient Signs of Kingship.

It was the will of their father that they should consult the Grand Vizier Nizam al Mulk for as long as he lived, and appoint another mutual Grand Vizier upon his death, so that none would have partisan advice in the last resort. Their father's last command had been this: that his sons should never take up arms against each other or any of their descendants, and that his sons and their descendants should always come to each other's aid in times of trouble. The sheikh's dying curse would be upon the head of any who violated this command, and upon his descendants for seven generations.

So the three princes grew to maturity under the eye of the old queen and the vizier, who did their best to prepare the princes for the future. When they reached the age of twenty-five, they came into their inheritance. Then each prince took his own Sign of Kingship and departed to his own palace and his own kingdom, where they lived in peace and accord with one another, as their father had commanded.

To Prince Karim's lot fell the seaside palace of the country now called West Barakat, and the protection of the Great Jewel Seal of Shakur. This emerald seal, made for an ancient king of the lineage, was the subject of a legend that warned that if the Seal were lost, the kingdom would be lost. Karim knew that his people were superstitious, and that he must ever guard and keep the Seal if he valued his kingdom.

One

October 1994

"**A** historic moment in the Barakat Emirates today," the NewsBreakers anchorman announced. "A landmark agreement, opening the Emirates to foreign investment for the first time in modern history, is being signed this morning by the representatives of four countries and the three new Barakati princes. In a few moments, NewsBreakers will take you live to the capital of the Barakat Emirates for the ceremony of signing. Except for a few diplomats over the centuries, this marks the first time that Westerners have seen inside the historic palace." He turned to his partner. "It's going to be quite an occasion, Marta."

"Yes, Barry, it is! Barakat has been virtually closed to Western interests for most of the past two centuries. Even the old sheikh, who was relatively modern in his views, restricted foreign investment and even tourism throughout a reign that began in 1937, effectively cutting Barakat off from the modern world. When he died—''

''Marta, sorry to interrupt, I think we're going live now—to the palace in the capital, Barakat al Barakat, where television cameras have been allowed into the Throne Room for the first time in history. Paul, are you there?''

''Hello, Barry, yes, the representatives of the Four Nations are already at the signing table as you see, and we've just had word that the princes are on their way,'' a reporter's voice murmured, over the image of a magnificent marble hall filled with milling dignitaries. ''At this moment they have apparently just left the private apartments and are making their way to the Throne Room along a corridor— it's called the Corridor of Decision—that their ancestors have used on state occasions since this palace was built in 1545. They will enter the Throne Room by the huge double doors that you see in the centre of the screen, behind the signing table. That's the massive Lion Throne to the right of the doors.''

''Massive seems to be an understatement,'' said Marta.

''We tried to get some statistics on the value and weight of the throne, Marta, and what kind of baubles are embedded in it, but the habit of secrecy...all right, the doors are opening now—those doors are being opened, by the way, by high courtiers, not by menials, and it's a task they vie for—and first through the door, we've been briefed, will be the Grand Vizier Nizam al Mulk, the favorite advisor of the last sheikh and joint Regent during the minority of the princes, which ended only last year...and there he is! The Grand Vizier of the Barakat Emirates.''

A white-bearded old man of impressive dignity, his costume sparkling with jewels, was seen walking through the great doorway. He paused briefly and moved down the steps towards the table below.

Paul murmured, ''That, we're told, is the traditional ceremonial dress of the Grand Vizier on state occasions, but you can believe the princes' own regalia will put his in the shade. And of course the aura of power you sense is just that. Nizam was the Regent for seven years, his regency ending only last year, as I said, and he still has the very important role of advisor to all three princes.

''Just behind him are coming now the Prime Minister and the members of the Cabinet, all elected officials. Barakat is what they call a democratic monarchy...and following them, twelve men who hold the ceremonial office still called the Cup Companions, looking very magnificent in their own fabulous ceremonial robes. By tradition the king has twelve Cup Companions, and I believe each of the three princes does still appoint twelve, but to...ah, limit the formality of the occasion, we're told,'' Paul said dryly, ''a representative joint twelve has been chosen on this occasion.

''And a dramatic pause, of course, because the next to appear—they will step over the threshold neatly abreast to show that they share power equally—will be the three princes themselves.

''And there they are!'' In spite of a jaded outlook and, in the course of fifteen years in television news, having seen it all, Paul could not keep the excitement from his voice.

''Oh my God!'' exclaimed Marta involuntarily. She had been anchorwoman only two years and had not quite attained the ideal of journalistic impassivity.

Across the threshold into the ancestral Throne Room stepped the three princes, equal but very individual exemplars of regal bearing, handsome countenance, and staggering magnificence. Those watching, both in the Throne

Room and in front of their television sets, fell unconsciously silent for a few telling seconds.

"Well, if you'd asked me, I would have said it wasn't
possible in the modern age," said Barry faintly, and in
Barakat Paul merely murmured, "Yes, I think words would
be superfluous here. That is a truly breathtaking sight."

Framed by the graceful decorated arch of the ancient
entrance, the three princes paused, smiling at the applaud-
ing crowd in the room below. Dressed in coats of heavy
cloth of gold, trousers of gold-embroidered silk, and rings
and necklaces studded with glittering jewels and glowing
pearls, each also wore a magnificent and unusual turban of
pleated cloth of gold, each adorned with a central jewel the
size of a fist—one ruby, one emerald, one sapphire.

A camera angled for a closeup of all three at once, for
the handsome faces, individually quite different, together
seemed to present almost the embodiment of masculine
beauty. Prince Omar, with his broad forehead, thin, aristocratic cheeks, haughty green eyes and neat beard, Prince
Rafi, as handsome as a Persian miniature painting, with a
dark mustache, and Prince Karim, with the clean-shaven
dark good looks of an ancient desert warrior. They left no
doubt as to their masculine as well as their political power.

"What a trio! Strong women are fainting all over this
country as I speak," Marta opined.

"Those three faces, as you see them there, with their
ceremonial turbans, decorate every piece of money in the
three kingdoms," Paul told the viewers. "There is a communal currency as well as a central Parliament in the Emirates. Karim on the left, wearing the sapphire on his turban,
rules West Barakat, Rafi in the centre, under the ruby, is
the Emir of East Barakat, and Omar is the ruler of Central
Barakat. Those are the divisions their father made when,
like King Lear, he divided his kingdom so that all his sons

should inherit. It has worked better than King Lear's arrangement, though, it has to be said."

"How old are the princes, Paul?"

"They all turn twenty-six next week, Marta, but in case any of our female viewers is thinking about throwing herself in front of their horses, I should point out that Prince Omar is already married and has two young children."

"But it's open season on Prince Rafi and Prince Karim?"

"You can safely put on your hunting jacket for them, Marta."

As one, the three princes moved forward and down the red carpeted marble steps to the signing table as the ranks of the world's photographers parted before them. The members of the Four Nations, looking oddly plain in black dinner suits, stepped forward, and all shook hands with one other.

"If you're interested," Paul said, "that's a total of seventeen handshakes taking place there now, but of course, it's all going on simultaneously, in keeping with the strict public protocol that keeps the princes equal."

At the long, polished black table, six men and a woman took their seats in a row facing the cameras of the world. In front of each place was a large closed book, its gold cover embossed with the insignia of Barakat, the mythical bird called the Senmurgh.

"Now each of the signatories to the agreement will sign each of the seven books and take one home," Paul explained. Onscreen seven assistants could be seen like a small troupe of dancers in an almost perfectly choreographed grapevine step, picking up a book after each signature and weaving through his or her partners in the dance to place it in front of the next dignitary. "This, by the way, is what's referred to here as 'approval in the Western tradition.' By tradition it is not considered binding for a Sheikh of Barakat merely to sign a document.''

At the end, to another gentle round of applause from courtiers and observers, the seven assistants, each clutching a book, bowed to the table and moved to one side of the Throne Room.

''And now for the ceremony without which no treaty or state document has been legal in Barakat for hundreds of years,'' said Paul. ''No document is binding on any Barakat monarch until the monarch has stamped the document with the Great Jewel Seal of Shakur and drawn the Sword of Rostam over it, and finally, all the signatories have drunk from the Cup of Jalal.

''All of these ancient items have been the property of the Barakat royal house for six hundred years or more. In addition to dividing the kingdom, Sheikh Daud's will decreed that his sons should each individually inherit one of what are, for their subjects at least, powerfully evocative symbols of monarchy.''

A large ivory-colored parchment was now carried by the Grand Vizier to a marble table that stood to one side of the Lion Throne, placed on it, and unrolled. It was covered with ornate Arabic calligraphy of the highest quality, and, with its gold leaf and beautiful ink colours, resembled, to the Western audience, nothing so much as a page from a medieval illuminated Bible. It was held in place with two flat heavy sticks of ivory.

A courtier moved to stand beside the Grand Vizier, holding a small jar on a gold-and-silver engraved tray. Nizam al Mulk lifted the tiny golden urn and tilted it over the parchment. A thick, viscous red substance formed a pool in the centre of the top of the document.

Silence fell as Prince Karim approached. Just above his elbow the Great Jewel Seal of Shakur clung to his arm like a massive bracelet. He drew it off, then pressed the seal's face firmly into the pool of sealing wax on the parchment paper. When he lifted the seal again it had left behind the impression of a raised profile portrait of a crowned head. With a glance at the red seal and another at the Jewel, he restored the seal to its place on his arm.

"That's Prince Karim making the most of that particular ceremony," Paul informed his audience in an even lower murmur now, as though impressed in spite of himself. "The portrait is of Sultan Shakur, the direct ancestor of the three princes, who died about 1030, and the inscription surrounding the head reads in part, 'Great King, Sun of the Age, the Full Moon, World Conqueror, World Burner, the Throne of Mercy, the Sword of Justice, Defender of the Faith' and a lot more. The entire bracelet was cut by a master craftsman from a single giant emerald. And, Marta, it weighs almost two pounds!"

"Oooh!" The anchorwoman shivered with affected greed. "Must be worth a king's ransom!"

"Its worth is literally incalculable, because there is nothing else in the world to compare it to. The weight of the jewel alone puts it out of reach of most of us, but add to that the work of the sculpture—which is said, by those who have been privileged to study the ancient documents of this country, to be miraculously lifelike and artistic—and its value as a completely unique thousand-year-old artefact, and you're looking at what they call 'inestimable value.' I asked three jewellers for a ballpark figure, and the closest I could get was—in open auction, the sky's the limit.

"Now, there's Prince Rafi, I believe, stepping forward. He will draw the sword over the document, and then lay the naked steel right across the parchment," Paul murmured helpfully, as Prince Rafi did just that.

"The origins of that ritual are lost in the mists of time,

and although it is now said to symbolize the monarch's determination to defend a treaty with arms if necessary, it is thought by some that there was once another symbolism attached to it. Certainly it is true that if Prince Rafi were to draw the Sword of Rostam through the seal it would render the agreement instantly invalid. If he draws it against an enemy it signals a fight to the death.''

"How on earth do they keep track of all these customs?'' Marta marvelled.

"Don't forget they haven't changed for a millennium. And now the Cup of Jalal is brought forward,'' Paul spoke over her, "and now it's Prince Omar's turn. He will drink from the cup, sometimes called the Cup of the Soul, which is said by tradition to guarantee happiness to its owner, and then offer it to the signatories of the Four Nations, and lastly to his brothers. There's the Grand Vizier Nizam al Mulk carrying the cup to the foreign leaders—the contents, by the way, are a dark secret. Only the signatories will ever know what they drank—that's meant to be another form of protecting the treaty. And now Prince Rafi is drinking, and Prince Karim.

"And that is what is called 'sealing in the Barakati tradition,' so this historic agreement has now been formally signed and sealed, Marta, in one of the most impressive marriages of Eastern and Western tradition in modern times.''

Two

"**W**ill Mr. David Percy and Miss Caroline Langley please meet their driver at the Information Desk. Will Mr. Percy and Miss Langley—"

Caroline was hot. They had been left standing in the Royal Barakat Air plane for twenty minutes after something went wrong with the doors, but that hadn't stopped the captain turning off the air conditioning. Then there had been an endless wait before the luggage from their flight made its appearance on the mile-long conveyor belt, and everyone had been pressing so close that Caroline—with a new appreciation of what it meant to say that people from the Middle East had a smaller "personal territory" than Westerners—had found it impossible to see her own bags till they were half the arrivals hall away. While she was wrestling them off the belt someone had filched her trolley, and rather than hunt down another one, she had simply carried her bags, a mistake she would not make again soon in an inadequately air-conditioned building.

Her neat white linen travel suit was smudged, damp and badly creased, her skin was beaded with sweat all over her body, her makeup was history, her short honey-gold hair now clustered in unruly curls around her head, her always volatile temper was in rags.

It didn't help to know that if David had been with her, her arrival in this little-known country would have been very different. The smell of money generally ensured that for David things ran smoothly. But at the last minute David had called to say that he could not make the trip—and Caroline had come alone.

She had not really been surprised when David cancelled. She had almost been expecting it. There was something about this trip that David hadn't liked right from the beginning. He had even tried to talk her out of buying the raffle ticket.

"I've never yet met anyone who won a raffle, Caroline," he had said with raised eyebrows, as though the only reason for parting with money must be in the hope of getting a return.

"Well, it's for a charity, David," she had smiled pacifically, pulling out the few dollars that was the price of three tickets. They were being sold in aid of a hospital being built in the Barakat Emirates. "I don't mind not winning."

He picked up the ticket stub. "The Queen Halimah Hospital, Barakat al Barakat!" he read with derision. "Do you really believe that your money is actually going towards such a purpose?"

But she had already taken out the money, and the child selling the tickets—by the pool at the exclusive club where

David was a member—had said indignantly, "Yes, it is! They're building a new children's wing!" And she had passed the money over and written her name and phone number on three pale green tickets.

When she won, it had been a small triumph of feeling over logic. She had been thrilled with her prize—a first class, all-expenses-paid visit to the new resort in West Barakat—but she had managed to damp down her excitement before telling anyone about it. David no more liked to see evidence of her volatile nature and easily touched feelings than did her parents. He had predicted a chaotic holiday where nothing ran on time, but he had agreed to come along.

When he had cancelled, only a few hours before their flight, he had made it clear he expected Caroline to give it up, too. It was too late for her to invite anyone else along in his place, and he was sure she would not want to go to a somewhat remote Islamic country on her own. He would take her "somewhere equally exotic" within a week or two.

But Caroline, unusually for her, had dug her heels in.

"Oh, darling, are you sure you should?" her mother had asked nervously, but Caroline had gone on packing.

"The condemned man ate a hearty meal, Mother," she said. "I'm sick and tired of holidays paid for by someone else. I won this, it's my holiday, and I'm going to take it," she said. For years now they had been entirely dependent on someone else for everything, Caroline impatiently felt, and she hated it.

Caroline's parents had been born into East Coast aristocracy. Both had generations of breeding, wealth and influence behind them. But Thomas Langley had not inherited the business brain of his forebears, nor, more fatally, the wit to recognize the fact. On the advice of his son, he

had attempted to shore up his failing business with investment in the junk bond market during the eighties. When
that bubble burst, his son had died late one night as his car
hit a bridge. No one said the word except the insurance
company, but even if the policy *had* paid the double in-
demnity due in cases of accident, the money would have
been a drop in the sea of Thom Langley Senior's mounting
debts. And he had followed that catastrophe with a steady
string of bad decisions that had finally wiped him out.

Those terrible years had naturally taken a disastrous toll
on Caroline. She was a straight-A's student, but her marks
had gone into instant decline in the months after Thom
Junior's suicide. She had won no scholarships, and she certainly wouldn't have been accepted to any of the top uni-
versities she had once confidently dreamed of attending.

But she wasn't going to university anyway. It was one
thing for her parents to live on family handouts, and her
sister Dara was still in high school; it was another thing
entirely for Caroline. In spite of protests from her long-
suffering uncles that there was of course no objection to
paying for Caroline's education, she had declined to apply
for university and had taken a job.

She had wanted to leave home at the same time, but her
mother had begged her to stay on in the family mansion,
the one thing to have survived the disaster. Her salary
helped against the ridiculous expense of running the place,
her domestic labours increasingly helped make up for de-
parting servants, and her presence seemed to give her
mother "moral comfort, darling."

If she had stuck to her plans to go, she would never have
met David.

There were several men striding up and down in front
of the Information Desk when she got there, and she eyed

them with a sinking heart as she approached. Most were jingling car keys. There wasn't one who looked like someone she cared to entrust her health and safety to; young and fleshy, with their strutting self-importance, they looked too heedless to be chauffeurs.

The men stood aside to let her approach the desk, eyeing her with a wet-eyed interest as if hoping she was their fare and wondering what kind of tip they could extort from her.

"My name is Caroline Langley," she said, when the woman behind the desk turned to give her her attention. "You paged me."

"Ah, yes!" said the young woman, consulting her pad. "Your driver is here, Miss Langley...where did he go? Oh, yes, there!" She smiled and pointed, and Caroline, following her gesture, gasped slightly as her eyes fell on a man who was not in the least like the others.

He was well-built, tall, with an air of purpose and decision, and an unconsciously aristocratic bearing that would have put David in the shade. He stood by a pillar, quietly talking to another man. Caroline blew a damp curl out of her eye and smiled involuntarily just with the pleasure of looking at him.

His hair was dark and cut close against a well-shaped head, his wide, well-shaped mouth not quite hidden by a neatly curling black beard. Big as he was, there seemed to be not a spare ounce of flesh on his frame. Except for the beard, he looked like a glossy magazine photo of a polo player. He had straight, heavy black eyebrows, and curling black lashes clustered thickly around eyes that now, as if intuitively, rested on Caroline.

She smiled; he frowned. Then, under his lowered eyebrows, his dark eyes widened in an intent look, his gaze questioning, and more than questioning. Caroline shivered with awareness of his sheer physical presence and unconsciously drew herself up straighter, her shoulders back, as if he were a threat. As if his look was a challenge and she must not show any sign of weakness.

He spoke to his companion, who also whirled to stare at her, and left him standing by the pillar as he moved to approach her. "Miss Langley?" he enquired in a deep, strong voice that, except for a certain throaty emphasis on the consonants, had little trace of accent. "Miss Caroline Langley?"

She had the craziest urge to deny it, and run. The smile faltered on Caroline's lips, but she submitted to the human reluctance to make a scene on inadequate grounds. "Are you from the hotel?" she temporized.

"Not precisely the hotel, but rather the Royal Barakat Tour Agency. My name is Kaifar, Miss Langley. I am your personal guide. It is my job to liaise for you and your fiancé with the hotel and all the other sites you choose to visit to make sure that your trip is an enjoyable one."

"I see." His voice was deep and warm, rippling along her nerves. Perhaps it was just being alone in a very unfamiliar country that made her so nervous, not his presence at all.

"Your fiancé, Mr. Percy—where is he?" he continued. "He has been detained at Customs?"

His gaze was clear and steady. He was a very good-looking man. She swallowed. "David had to cancel, I'm afraid. I'm here alone."

The strong black eyebrows snapped together. "He did not come?" He was frowning almost fiercely, his gaze piercing her, yet why should he be angry? It must be a cultural misunderstanding. Or perhaps in his experience women were not such good tippers.

"David couldn't make it. Is there a problem with my being on my own here?" She had been told that the Barakat

Emirates were secular and moderate, but maybe as an un-accompanied woman she should be wearing chador or have a chaperone or something. She hoped not.

He laughed at her, his teeth white against the black beard, charismatic as a fairy-tale brigand. "Certainly not!" he assured her. "I am merely surprised. I was prepared to pick up two people. One moment."

He moved over beside the man to whom he had been speaking a minute ago and spoke a few words in a language she took to be Arabic. The companion flicked her a glance, and then began to argue. But the chauffeur merely held up his hand and said something in a very autocratic manner, and his companion fell silent, shaking his head. The man named Kaifar returned to her.

"My companion will bring your bags." At his request Caroline pointed to where her luggage sat. "Follow me. Please," he added as an afterthought, and with an arm not quite touching her he guided her through the thronging mass of humanity and baggage that was between them and the door.

And then, with her dark guide beside her, Caroline stepped out of the airport into the heat and beauty of the exotic, exciting, little-known land that was called, in the language of its people, Blessing.

Kaifar led her to a vintage Rolls Royce and installed her in the back seat while the other man stowed her luggage. The two men spoke together for a moment, then bid each other farewell as Kaifar climbed into the driver's seat. But instead of starting the car, he sat for a long moment, stroking his beard, his eyes shuttered, deep in thought. Caroline shivered.

She leaned forward abruptly. "What is the problem?"

He came out of his trance in some surprise, and looked

haughtily over his shoulder at her, as if she had no right to question his actions. Caroline thought dryly, *Well, if West Barakat wants to attract tourists, the guides are going to have to get used to women who know what they want.*

But his next words indicated that he was already aware of that. "I beg your pardon, Miss Langley," he said with a brief nod.

She felt a sensation of unease that she could not pinpoint. Belatedly she saw that she had only Kaifar's word for it that he had been officially sent to pick her up. She had seen no identification. And he was not in uniform, merely a white shirt and dark trousers. He could be anyone. She thought about his reaction to the news that David had not come. He spoke good English—he might easily have discovered that David was rich. Suppose he was planning something?

"Where are you taking me?" she challenged, realizing that she was in a position from which it would now be almost impossible to escape. Why hadn't she asked him for some I.D. inside?

He leaned forward and pressed the car into life. He spoke over his shoulder without turning his head to look at her as the car moved forward.

"I am taking you to your hotel, where else?" he said shortly.

"What is the name of the hotel?" she said, but it was too little, too late if her nameless fears were right. The car was already picking up speed.

He smiled in the mirror at her, looking like nothing so much as a desert bandit in a fairy tale. "The name of the hotel is the Sheikh Daud, Miss Langley. It is on the Royal Road that runs near the coast to the west of the city. Please calm your fears. Not all dark Arabs are desert sheikhs carrying off beautiful women to their harems. Some of us are so civilised we would even consider many of your own compatriots barbarian.''

His teeth looked white and strong behind the black beard. He seemed to be inviting her to smile with him at her own foolish, unfounded nervousness. Kaifar slowed the car and turned out of the airport onto a wide, palm-lined boulevard, and this might be her last chance to leap out of the car. Caroline tensed.

Kaifar turned slightly to look at her. ''You will find the hotel very pleasant, Miss Langley. It is the best and most exclusive hotel in the Barakat Emirates. You were very lucky to win such a prize, yes?''

She felt the buzz of his smile, the impact of the arrogant, effortless masculinity against her feeble guard, and thought, *Is that what I'm afraid of? The fact that he's so masculine and sexy?*

Maybe she should have listened to David. Maybe it had not been wise to come on her own. She had suspected that there was something David was worried about, though he had denied it. Had it been a fear that she would fall for some attractive foreigner?

Someone like Kaifar.

The airport was northeast of the city. ''Shall I tell you about our country as we pass?'' Kaifar enquired. He waved a hand and, without waiting for an answer, began pointing out the sights to her: an ancient ruined fortress almost buried by blown sand; a wadi in the distance, palm trees against golden dunes; a small desert village, looking as though it were still in the Iron Age, except for the single satellite dish.

''That is the house of the chief man of the village. Once the possession of two mules marked his wealth. Now it is a television set,'' he told her, smiling again. Yet she couldn't relax.

Soon they were in the city. The car entered a large leafy square, and a fabulously decorated, magical building of blue mosaic tile and mirrored glass came into view. "This is our Great Mosque," he said grandly. "It was built in the fifteenth and sixteenth centuries by m—" he paused, as if seeking the name "—Queen Halimah. Her tomb also is here."

Caroline gazed at it, entranced by her first live sight of such exotic beauty. After a glance at her rapt face, Kaifar slowed the car and drew in at the curb. The broad stone-paved courtyard was shaded by trees and cooled by fountains, and she watched the people—tourists and the worshippers together—strolling about. The place cast a spell of peace. A sense of wonder crept over her at the magnificence of the architecture, followed by a curious feeling of recognition. Her mouth opened in a little gasp.

"What is it, Miss Langley?"

"I think my fiancé has a miniature of this scene, painted on ivory! Is that possible?" How different, how unimaginably more impressive the place was in real life.

"Anything is possible, is it not? That a man in New York should have a miniature of such a building is not very astonishing, even if one wonders why he wants it. Has your fiancé visited my country?"

"I don't think so. No."

"Yet he wants a painting of the Great Mosque."

"My fiancé is a collector."

Kaifar was silent.

"An antiques collector, you know," she said, thinking he might not understand the term. "He buys ancient works of art and...objects. Mostly Greek and Roman, but he does have some oriental things."

"Ah, he *buys* them?" He stuck his arm out the window to wave an old man on a wobbling bicycle past. In the bicycle basket she was fascinated to see a dirty, battered computer monitor.

She smiled at his naivete. "How else could he collect them?"

He shrugged. "People have things that have been given to them. Or that they have stolen."

Caroline bristled. "I am quite sure that David has paid for everything in his collection," she said coldly. "Believe me, he is rich enough to buy the whole mosque, he doesn't have to—"

His voice cut harshly across hers. "No one is rich enough to buy the Great Mosque. It is not for sale." He sounded furious, and Caroline could have kicked herself. She didn't want to make an enemy of her guide before her trip had even begun. Some foreigners, she knew, were offended by the casual assumption that everything, including their heritage, had a price.

"I'm sorry. I didn't mean that literally. Of course such a thing would never be for sale," she said hastily.

Kaifar turned his head. "They come in the night, and they steal the treasures of the mosques and museums— even, they chip away the ancient tiles and stone monuments. Now we have a guard on many sites, and those who make the attempt and are caught are put in prison. But it is impossible to guard everything, and the danger only puts the price so high that someone can always be found to make the attempt. This is what foreign collectors do to my country's heritage."

Caroline was hot with a sense of communal guilt. "I'm sure David's never done anything like that!"

"Are you?" he asked, as if the subject already bored him. "Well, then, we must not blame your fiancé for our troubles."

In fact she knew nothing at all of David's business practices. She said, as her father might have done, "Anyway, if people are willing to pillage their own heritage for money, that's hardly the fault of the buyer, is it?"

He hit the brakes at an orange light so that she was flung forward against the seat belt, but when she looked in the mirror his face was impassive, and his voice when he spoke was casual.

"You yourself have no experience of what desperate things people will do for money?"

She stared at him as a slow, hot blush crept up under her skin. It was impossible, she told herself. His remark could not have been meant ironically—he probably believed she was rich. But he had scored a bull's-eye.

Caroline had many feelings about her engagement, but never, until this moment, had she felt shame. Shame that she should be allowing David to buy her, a human being, exactly as he bought the pieces for his collection. And for just the reason Kaifar cited—because of desperation for money.

Three

Twenty minutes later she was standing in a cool, comfortable room, looking out through a glass door onto a shaded balcony and the sea beyond.

"You will want to relax, have a drink, bathe and change," Kaifar informed her, waving at the terrace where he had instructed a porter to place a tray of ice and drinks. "I will return for you in three hours. Then we will have dinner."

She frowned in surprise. "What do you mean? Why are you taking me to dinner?"

He shrugged. "I am a part of your prize, Miss Langley," he said, with a smile that made her turn nervously away. "Would you like to go to a European restaurant, or do you prefer to try the foods of my country?"

What was she complaining about? She certainly didn't want to dine alone. "Well, then, the food of the country, thank you."

Kaifar nodded once and withdrew, leaving her on her own. Caroline went to the exotically arched patio door, drew it open, and stepped out onto terra cotta tiles delicately interspersed with a pattern in white and blue. She sighed in deep satisfaction. How good it was to get away, to be alone, to think. She seemed to have had no time for thinking since her father had first told her of David's offer.

Far in the distance, scarcely discernible, a muezzin was calling the faithful of the city to prayer. Ahead of her stretched the fabulous blue waters of the Gulf of Barakat. Palm trees, planted in the courtyard below, stretched up to the vaulted, pillared canopy that protected half the terrace from the sun. There were plants everywhere her eye fell. A table and chairs nestled against the trunk of one of the trees, and Caroline sank down, dropped ice into a glass, and poured herself some mineral water.

The surroundings were so soothing. Her troubles and responsibilities seemed miles away. She had no choices to make, no unpleasant facts to face, tasks to perform. She was facing two weeks where she need please no one save herself.

Sayed Hajji Karim ibn Daud ibn Hassan al Quraishi reached a deceptively lazy hand out to the bowl of glistening fruit and detached a grape. He examined the grape, his curving lids hiding the expression in his eyes. The fruit was plump and purple-black, but not nearly as deeply dark as the monarch's angry eyes, a fact which Nasir could verify a moment later, when Prince Karim slipped the juicy globelet between his white teeth and raised his piercing gaze to his secretary.

"In truth, Lord, no one save yourself and Prince Rafi and I know what your intentions are. Who could have revealed them? Only I myself have knowingly been engaged in the execution of these plans. The truth has been disguised from all the others. All has been as secretly done as you ordered, Lord.''

"And yet he did not come," said Prince Karim.

The secretary bowed. "If I may speak plainly," he began, but he scarcely paused for the permission the ritual question implied. He was a trusted advisor and he spoke freely in conference with his prince. "This may easily be the action of a guilty man who fears some nameless coincidence, or a busy man contemptuous of the arrangements and desires of others. It is not necessarily the action of a man who has been warned of trouble.''

"He is a man who subverted one of my own staff," Karim said flatly. The monotone did not fool the secretary. Prince Karim advertised his anger only when there was something to be gained from a show of royal rage.

The secretary bowed his head. "True, Lord. By my eyes, he has not subverted me.''

Prince Karim lifted a hand. "No such suspicion has crossed my mind, Nasir.''

Prince Rafi spoke. "Good! Then we must operate on the assumption that there has been no leak of information, and alter our plans to suit the circumstance. All is not yet lost! The woman is here, after all!''

The sun set as she waited; the air was cooler, and a breeze moved beguilingly across the terrace. The transformation from light to dark happened quickly, a bucket of molten gold dropping down into the navy ocean and drawing after it night and a thousand stars. Now the world was magical.

She was waiting, half for Kaifar, half for a phone call to go through. She had tried and failed to call David earlier, then had given up, showered and dressed. She was wearing a green cotton sundress with wide straps and a bodice cut not too low across her breasts; a gauzy, gold-shot scarf patterned in greens with pinks and blues and yellows would cover her shoulders if necessary. Her hair was clean and obedient again, swept back from her forehead and neck as smoothly as the vibrant natural curls would allow. She wore a gold chain, gold studs, and her engagement ring.

Caroline had been absolutely astonished when her father had approached her with David Percy's proposal of marriage. She hardly knew the man, although she was aware that he was a friend of her father's, an antiques dealer and collector who had sold Thom Langley a few things in the old days. They had met only once or twice. She believed then that he had fallen in love with her from a distance, and she had been ready to laugh with her father over David's middle-aged foolishness.

Then she had seen that her father wanted her to marry David Percy. And when her mother came in, Louise had made no effort to pretend her husband had not already informed her of the great news. "Oh, Caroline, isn't it a miracle! Who would have thought that a man like David Percy would want *you!*" she had burst out with such relief and gratitude in her tone that Caroline understood that for both of them David Percy's offer represented a salvation worth any sacrifice. Even a daughter's happiness.

"But Mother, he's so—" Caroline stopped, because she couldn't find the words to describe the awful coldness that she felt from David. Worse, much worse, than her own father's.

Thomas Langley had always disapproved of his elder daughter's "emotional extremes," her capacity for deep feeling and unguarded responses, so unlike his own nature or even that of his wife's. Whether she was touched by the plight of a stray cat in a Caribbean resort, or moved to tears by a painting in an Italian church, her father frowned. Caroline had grown up under the constant pressure to contain her laughter, restrain her tears, to walk sedately and talk quietly.

"Darling, it's not forever," Louise had hastily assured her. She had talked fast, not giving Caroline time to express objections. "David won't expect you to stay married to him for long. He knows better than that. You'll be divorced by the time you're thirty!"

Caroline shuddered. "And who will get custody of the children?"

"Darling, you're looking for problems! David may not even want children. And at thirty, look where you'll be. You'll have serious money—you can trust your father to see to that—and you probably won't look a day older than you do now. The cosmetic aids you'll be able to afford! The massage, the clinics! Whereas I'm aging a little more with every day that passes."

"Being eternally young isn't really high on my list of priorities," Caroline responded dryly, but her mother overrode her.

"Caroline, you'll have money. Don't underestimate it. Money is the power to do whatever you like. You will have total freedom, Caroline." She emphasised each word of the last sentence.

Caroline had frowned as something whispered in the back of her mind that she would have total freedom now if she left her parents to the fate which their own foolish actions and constant living beyond their means had brought upon them.

And as though she sensed that, Louise had added quickly, with a pathetic catch to her voice, "*We'll* have freedom, too, Caroline. You can purchase our freedom as no one else can. And think of Dara. She'll be able to go to university, and I know you want her to be able to do that...."

But she would not have agreed to the engagement if she had not believed that David wanted to marry her because he loved her.

David had begun taking her to museums to introduce her to his way of life and her future, and one fine day he had introduced her to "herself"—a marble bust thought to be Alexander the Great. And that was when she discovered just what it was about his fiancée that David loved: Caroline looked like a Greek statue.

In profile her broad forehead sloped down into a finely carved nose with scarcely any change in angle; her slim eyebrows, set low, followed the line of her large, wide-spaced, grey eyes; her cheeks and jaw, though delicately moulded, curved with a fullness that was nothing like the fashionable gaunt hollowness of a Vogue model; her upper lip was slender and beautifully drawn, her lower lip full, curving up at the corners. And in addition there was the riot of curls over her well-shaped head and down the back of her neck. Her only flaw, if you were looking for physical perfection, was the slightly crooked front tooth.

The bust was, in fact, eerily like her. She was looking at her own death mask—or, she told herself, because the sculptor had been a great artist and the statue was certainly "alive," herself frozen in the mirror of time.

David had insisted on buying her a wardrobe suited to her new position as his fiancée. Caroline by then had felt out of control of events; she had been unable to protest at the arrangement, let alone the way that David dictated her choices. She had some very smart, and rather original, ivory and cream outfits in her wardrobe now. And a gold upper arm bracelet and heavy gold necklace that had cost as much as her year's salary.

When he had effected a certain amount of transformation, David threw a midsummer masquerade party to celebrate the public announcement of their engagement. For that he had designed Caroline's costume himself. Or, had hired a designer to execute what he wanted.

And what he wanted was Caroline looking as much like a Greek statue as possible. Intricately pleated ivory silk toga with flowing folds, ivory leather sandals, a wreath of ivory-coloured leaves in her hair, her skin painted to look like marble...when she stood perfectly still, she really had almost looked like marble.

"Don't smile with your teeth tonight, Caroline," David had ordered, with no apology for his air of command. "It spoils the illusion. Serenity, my dear." It was then that she had finally put all the pieces together. David did not love her. He didn't even imagine that he did. What he wanted was to add her to his collection. He wanted to own her.

In that moment she wondered whether it would be possible to recover from the personality changes David would exact from her.

A steady voice in her head had whispered, *Get out now. Tell him you've changed your mind, tell him not to make the announcement tonight.* But Caroline had stifled the thought. Her mother was right. A few years of sacrifice was not too much for her family to ask.

Of course, the couple's photograph had illustrated the story of the engagement in the newspaper. *David Percy Adds "The Jewel in the Crown" To His Private Collection* was the headline.

When she had learned, while she was in the midst of packing her bags for this trip, that David would not be coming, Caroline had taken out of her case all the clothes he had bought her and packed instead her own clothes, bought at a discount where she worked. She would not have much chance to wear them once she was married.

Caroline liked colour. She was fairly sure the ancient Greeks had, too. Lots of the statues she had seen during her recent crash course in classical art under David's tutelage had obviously once been painted in very bright, intense colours, and she had read somewhere that it was possible that even what David called "the elegant proportions of the Parthenon" had been covered in bright red and turquoise and gold leaf. And as for emotions, in the ancient legends the Greeks seemed anything but serene. Even their gods had been wildly passionate and overly emotional...but she did not put that point of view to David.

Caroline sighed and slipped into the present. David was not here now, and if the phone didn't ring soon, she wouldn't have to talk to him. She was suddenly wildly grateful that David had not come on this trip. He would have insisted on New York standards everywhere. She wanted to see, to experience the East, its beauty, its passion, its legendary contradictions.

"The woman is very much younger than he," Nasir reported. "It is said that he paid her father a large amount of money for her." He passed a faxed copy of a newspaper photograph to the two princes.

"'The jewel in his crown!'" Karim read the caption headline.

"Ah, a Mona Lisa!" exclaimed Prince Rafi with interest.

Karim gazed at the photo. It showed a pale, grave-eyed young woman in costume half smiling at someone beyond the camera, beside a smooth-skinned man of middle age. He looked up and met the eyes of his secretary. "And this is what he thinks of this woman?" he asked, indicating the headline. The secretary only bowed his head. "He adds her to his collection?" Karim pursued.

"Allowances must of course be made for the inaccuracies of gossip and the liberties taken by the press," the secretary offered diffidently.

Prince Karim nodded, his black eyes glittering. His face took on the harsh look of a desert tribesman riding to battle as he turned back to the photograph. "Excellent! It may be, then, that Mr. Percy would like to make an exchange."

Nasir showed no surprise, but nothing ever did surprise him.

"The jewel of my collection for the jewel of his," went on Prince Karim. "First, of course, we will have to gain possession of Mr. Percy's jewel."

When Kaifar appeared at her door, he was wearing a suit of white cotton trousers and shirt that was "neither of the East nor of the West" but looked as though it would be comfortable anywhere. But still, with his dark skin and black beard, he looked richly exotic to her eyes. On his strong bare feet he wore the kind of thong sandals that she had earlier noticed men and women in the city wearing.

They stood for a moment in the doorway, not speaking. Then Caroline dropped her gaze and said, "I'll get my bag." Her voice came out sounding weak, almost breathless. Leaving the door open, she turned and went back into the sitting room, where her scarf and evening bag lay on a chair.

The phone rang.

Kaifar stepped inside the room, closed the door, and picked up the receiver. For a moment he spoke in Arabic, then was silent, waiting.

Surprised at this autocratic action—had he given out her room number as a contact for himself?—Caroline frowned, but he smiled blandly at her and turned to speak into the mouthpiece. "Good evening, Mr. Percy! This is Kaifar speaking! We are very sorry that you are in New York and not here in our beautiful country."

Caroline gasped. "Give me the phone!" In two quick steps she was beside him. He was tall; her eyes were on a level with the curling black beard that covered his chin. "Give it to—" she began again, but an imperious hand went up and in spite of herself she was silenced.

Suddenly his teeth flashed in a wide grin, and she involuntarily fell back a step, as if a wolf had smiled. But the smile was not meant for her. "My name is Kaifar, Mr. Percy," he repeated with a curious emphasis. "Doubtless we shall speak again. In the meantime, here is Miss Langley."

"Hello, David," she said, taking the phone with a speaking look and then turning away as she pressed it to her ear.

"Caroline? Where are you, my dear?"

And she lied. When she should have said, *In my hotel suite,* out of a purely instinctive reaction she said instead, "In the lobby of the hotel, David." She had simply no idea how David would react to the thought of a strange foreigner in her hotel room answering her phone, and she shrank from knowing.

"And who was that man? I understood they were putting me through—"

"Kaifar is the guide whose services I won as part of the prize." There was a curious pause as the word "services" echoed slightly, and then David spoke again, as if he had decided to ignore whatever impact he had felt from her last statement.

"Did you have a good flight?"

"Very comfortable."

They chatted only a few moments, just long enough for

David to ascertain that she had arrived safely. Caroline never had very much to say to David, but she would have kept him if she could. She was suddenly afraid of what would happen when she put the phone down. But there was no way to prevent David bidding her a calm goodbye and hanging up.

Caroline held on to the phone for a long moment afterwards, pretending to listen, but at last she said a feeble goodbye to the dial tone and hung up.

Then she lifted her head and met Kaifar's eyes, knowing that the lie to David had been a terrible mistake.

He was staring at her. He said, "Your dress is the colour of the emeralds that come from the mines in the mountains of Noor. They are the most beautiful emeralds in the world."

The words struck her like an unexpected wave, leaving her breathless. The lamp cast chiaroscuro light and shadow on him, his face and his hands richly toned, perfectly painted by the master, his eyes mysterious as they watched her, the rest of him shadowed. She felt that the whole universe was waiting for something; as if her whole future might be written in the next moment. Nothing outside the circle of light that embraced them had any relevance.

Something she could not name seemed to course between them. Her gaze moved from his shadowed eyes to his hands, and then, drawn by the magnet of his focus, back up to his eyes again. Her breasts rose and fell with her shallow breathing. There was another rhythm, too, under those of heart and breath and feeling: a deeper, mysterious rhythm as of life itself.

In the silence he stepped around her to pick up her scarf. It fell gracefully in his grasp, the gold threads glittering in lamplighted shadow. Caroline's lips parted in a small, audible breath as he lifted his hands to drape it around her shoulders. His touch was sure but light. His hands did not pause to rest on her bare skin beneath the gauzy silk.

"This way, Miss Langley," he said, and opened the door.

Four

"We have surveillance?" Prince Karim asked Nasir.

"Three teams of two, Lord—at all times. Others as necessary. Forgive me, but even—you know such precautions are necessary."

Prince Karim nodded in absent agreement. "And all is prepared?"

"Everything is in readiness, Lord. Jamil has all in hand."

"You are leaving when?"

"Tomorrow, Lord, at first light."

She awoke restless and disturbed, wondering where she was, who she was, not knowing her own name. In a panic, she sat up, flailing for the lamp that must be near. She knew that much, that beside beds you found lamps.... Her eyes, growing accustomed to the darkness, sought out the glitter of stars through the patio door, and she staggered up and opened it.

By the time she felt the soft breeze caress her forehead she was fully awake. Caroline. She was Caroline Langley and she was on vacation in the Barakat Emirates. She was fully clothed; she must have fallen asleep on the sofa. She had sat there thinking for hours after Kaifar brought her back. She must have slipped down and dozed off. She had a vague memory of putting out the lamp. Her dream had woken her.

It was Kaifar's fault. Dining with him tonight had disturbed her. Just being with him oppressed her. With a shiver Caroline found the overhead light switch and pressed it, welcoming the assault of the too-bright light on her wide-open eyes.

He was like that, like the light. The pupils of her inner self's eyes were wide—looking for something?—and Kaifar was too bright, blinding her, unbalancing her. So she awoke without knowing her name....

He had put her in the back seat of the Rolls Royce limousine and driven her to the most wonderful restaurant—in a hidden courtyard, tables under sweet-smelling trees, the food utterly sensual, the darkness scarcely disturbed by the candlelight on each table. A white-haired old woman sitting in a corner had sung hauntingly, pure sounds that did not seem a human voice at all. She accompanied herself with a stringed instrument that entwined her song with tendrils of such beauty Caroline's heart contracted.

"What is she singing?" she finally whispered.

"She sings about love. About a man in love with his best friend's daughter. He fears to ask his friend for what he most desires, the girl for his wife."

Caroline's heart leapt painfully at the parallel, because David did not love her, and had not feared to ask for what he wanted.

"While he waits, the friend dies. In his will he leaves

him his parrot—and the guardianship of the very daughter whom the man loves.''

He paused, listening to the song. She wanted to smile, to say something light, but she felt locked inside herself, imprisoned by something she couldn't name.

'''Goodbye Marjan my wife, for instead you are my daughter.''' Kaifar, having caught up with the story, was translating in a low voice as the singer sang. He bent over the table towards her, speaking so softly she was forced to lean towards him, his voice for her ear alone. It was too intimate, but she could not draw back. '''A daughter does not become a wife. My love must be hidden even from my own eyes, from my heart.'''

"But why?" Caroline breathed.

Kaifar merely shook his head. "It is a matter of honour. As her guardian he may not take advantage of her."

"Oh," said Caroline. She wondered about her father's honour, about David's. The haunting song went on, with Kaifar's deep gentle voice a counterpoint.

"She came to him, she came at his request.
Whatever he asked Marjan, it was her pleasure to obey.
She smiled, white teeth and rosebud lips.
'What do you have to say to me?' she asked her father's dear friend.
'Marjan, my daughter,' he begins. 'Marjan.'
'Am I your daughter?' Marjan asks,
Smiling with white teeth and rosebud lips.
Her hair is a bouquet of blackness, petal on petal,
A night flower.
'Am I your daughter, are you my father?'
He hears the hidden message and turns away.
She puts her white hand on his sleeve.

'You are not my father, though I have loved you all
my life.
Though I love you best.'
'Marjan, your father must find a husband for you.
The time is right. I must find you a husband.'
The smile flees her rosebud lips.
'What husband do I need when I have you? I wish for
no husband.'''

The singer broke off, and the music built to a crescendo
and stopped. "It's not finished?" Caroline whispered,
hardly able to speak under the joint spell of her thoughts,
his words, the singer's voice and the music.

Kaifar sipped his wine. "No." The woman set aside her
instrument, rose to her feet and approached a nearby table.
A man gave her money, they exchanged a few words and
then she came to their table and Kaifar spoke with her and
gave her money, too.

Caroline was able to smile at last. "If she is paid enough,
she goes on with the story?" she joked gently.

"The storyteller's art has always partly involved knowing how to build to moments of tension and then stop."

Caroline smiled. "Scheherazade being the foremost ex-
ponent of the art?"

Kaifar nodded encouragingly.

The waiter brought them the first course, *naan* with fresh
green herbs and white goat's cheese and several other small
dishes that were unfamiliar to her. She tore off some of the
flat bread and, following Kaifar's lead, took a delicate sprig
of herb and rolled it in the bread. The freshness of the herb
exploded in her mouth.

"Do you know the ending?" she asked after a moment.
The singer was still moving from table to table.

"Everyone knows the ending. It is a famous story."

"Tell me how it ends."

Kaifar set down his *naan* and leaned forward on his elbows. He smiled, a warm smile; and she remembered the way he had spoken to her, looked at her earlier in her room. She drew back slightly, but Kaifar began speaking again in a low voice, and in spite of herself Caroline was drawn forward to put her ear closer to his mouth.

"Marjan tries to tell her father's friend that she loves him as a husband and not a father, but he pretends not to understand. Then she begs him to wait, not to marry her off yet. But he chooses a handsome young man to be her husband, and believing that her love is hopeless, she marries the man he has chosen for her. Her father's friend falls sick with unrequited love. Marjan visits him, but even on his deathbed he manages to keep his secret. When he dies, Marjan takes charge of the parrot that was, to the last, his companion. As she sits mourning the man she loved, the parrot recites the words it has heard so many times. 'Marjan! I die for love of you!' So Marjan discovers the truth."

Caroline was suffocating. Tears burned her eyelids and she couldn't speak, though it was stupid to be so affected by a story. "Why?" she whispered at last. "Why couldn't he tell her?"

Kaifar watched her with eyes as shadowy as the night. "He believed in his duty, perhaps. People betray love for many reasons, some good, some bad."

People betray love. Did he mean she was betraying love, marrying David? Was that why the story affected her so fiercely? David was her father's friend, but he did not love her, nor she him. How could that be a betrayal of love? There was no man she loved now, even if one day there might be.

No, a part of her whispered. *Not if you marry David.* This seemed clear to her suddenly, sitting here with Kaifar's eyes on her—eyes that saw everything, that showed her her own soul. Marriage to David would kill her heart, her ability to love deeply. How had she failed to see this? They were not asking merely for the sacrifice of a few years of her life. It might be the sacrifice of her heart's future.

As the singer resumed her mournful song, Caroline could not entirely hold back the tears. They spilled out, one by one, sparkling in the candlelight as they slipped down her cheeks and fell into the darkness.

She thought Kaifar did not notice that she wept. She hoped he did not, just as she had often hoped her father would not notice the tears of too much feeling he disapproved of. Caroline was expert in the art of soundless weeping, the surreptitious wiping away of her own tears.

"Why do you hide your tears from me?" Kaifar asked.

Her hand trembled. The question tore down her frail control. She gulped and swallowed convulsively. "I'm sorry to be so stupid!" she whispered. "It's just—it's the first time I've ever heard music like that."

"Do you apologize for having a heart that is touched by the music of my country?" Kaifar demanded.

Caroline closed her eyes and her body shook with a single sob of reaction. When she opened her eyes again, tears spangled on her lashes, so that Kaifar—dark, powerful, mysterious, and deeply, primitively attractive to her—was haloed with sparks of candlelight, and watching her.

Gently, almost absently, with an indescribable grace, he reached out to her cheek and caught a tear as it fell, on his finger. He lifted his finger to his own lips and took the tear on his tongue.

Had she been standing, the gesture would have knocked her to the ground. She would not have been more shaken if he had struck her. Caroline silently opened her mouth and lifted her head back, blinking up at the black silk sky, desperate for air.

Her reaction to him was too strong. It frightened her. His presence was undermining her and all the certainties of her life. She was emotionally vulnerable to him somehow, and she must control herself, and him. He must not be allowed to imagine—Caroline put a brake on her thoughts.

"What do—" She coughed, because the tears in her throat made it almost impossible to speak. "What do you think you're doing?" she demanded.

He looked at her in arrogant surprise. "What did you say?"

He sounded so haughty Caroline almost quailed. Well, she had heard that Middle Eastern men were strong on male supremacy. That didn't mean she had to swallow it. "Why did you do that?" she demanded in a low voice, her feelings disguised as angry intensity. "Why did you taste my tears?"

The look he gave her would have melted her even if she were the marble statue that David wanted. "She is singing about tears, Caroline. 'The tears of a beautiful woman whose heart is only for one man, her tears are not salt. They are wine reserved for the gods.'"

His words made her shiver, but she must not be weak. "Why do you want to know about my heart?" she challenged.

He smiled his brigand's smile and made no answer.

"The state of my heart is none of your business!"

He lifted a hand, palm up. There was a slight, shrugging inclination of his head to indicate that he accepted her point.

And then, childishly, stupidly, Caroline gave away her victory by asking, "What did they taste of?"

His dark eyebrows came down in astonished anger. "Do you ask me to tell you whether you love your fiancé?"

Caroline's grey eyes darkened as she struggled to regain her footing. "I doubt if anyone's tears actually taste of wine! If you tell me what my tears tasted like to you, that tells me more about you than about the state of my heart, doesn't it?"

She felt like a tennis player who has returned an almost impossible volley and scored. She couldn't help smiling her triumph at him, her eyes exaggeratedly open.

"And your question, too, tells me about the state of your heart even if the taste of your tears does not."

The sudden shift from triumph to disaster was too much for her. Caroline exploded into anger. "How dare you!"

"How dare I what? Point out to you that you have asked me whether you love your fiancé?"

"I didn't ask you any such thing!" Unbidden tears burned her eyes and overflowed onto her cheeks, and she dashed them away with impatient fingers. But they would not go away. Under the impact of the song, and the release of repressed feeling, the truth of her state was too strong for her.

"Oh, God, why did I come here?" Caroline cried softly, her elbows on the table, her head between her hands, hiding her tears, struggling for calm. For the first time, she was admitting to herself that she did not want to marry David. Yet how would her parents survive if she did not?

Her tears subsided at last, and wiping her cheeks on her napkin, Caroline lifted her head and sat up. At least no one around them was staring at her. She reached for another piece of *naan,* and forced herself to chew and swallow. After the first few bites, it became easier. Kaifar joined her, saying nothing.

The song ended with the singer crying, "Marjan! Mar-

jan! Marjan!'' her sobbing notes managing to suggest both
the croaking voice of the parrot and a heart in the act of
breaking. There was applause. The waiter appeared with
their main course, a cool breeze blew across the garden,
and Caroline sat up straighter and decided that she had
better make some things clear.

Her marinated, grilled garlic chicken looked mouth-wa-
tering. Lifting fork and knife, Caroline asked, ''Would you
have eaten here tonight if my fiancé had come with me on
this trip?''

His eyebrows flew up. ''I mean—'' She could feel herself blushing at her own awkwardness, when she had meant
to re-establish the business footing—she did not allow herself even to think of the phrase *class distinction*—between
them, however belatedly. ''I mean, do you always eat with
your clients?''

Three men got up from a neighbouring table and began
to dance to the singer's new song. Caroline involuntarily
turned to watch. They were very ordinary-looking middle-
aged men, wearing loose trousers and shirts rolled up at the
cuffs to expose brown forearms sprinkled with dark hair.
They waved their arms above their heads, their hips gyrat-
ing like belly dancers.

Not something a straight man in New York would be
caught dead doing, Caroline thought, but it was powerfully
and directly masculine and it appealed to her senses in a
very primitive way. There was some quality that Kaifar
shared with these men and with no one she knew back
home.

''Not many people wish for a full-time guide,'' he said,
bringing her back. ''Your case is different.''

She turned back to him. ''Why?''

''Because you have won a prize,'' he replied, as though
it were self-evident. ''I eat with you to enhance your en-

joyment of your holiday. A woman does not like to eat alone.''

Caroline blushed at the subtle suggestiveness of the words. She wondered if Kaifar was used to looking after the emotional and sexual as well as the social needs of his single female customers.

Kaifar meanwhile was eating with rich enjoyment, but not the attitude of one who rarely tastes such delicacies.

''Does the company pay for your meal, too?''

''Do you worry about my wallet?'' He smiled and raised his eyebrows.

She felt the presumptuousness of her question. Somehow he seemed able to wrongfoot her every time. ''I was only wondering,'' she muttered.

''Or perhaps you are wondering what other services are included with your prize?'' Kaifar's meaning was blatant now, his eyes suddenly reflecting powerful sexual interest as well as candlelight.

''Everything is included, Miss Langley,'' he promised softly as he gazed hypnotically into her eyes. ''You may ask for anything you desire. And you need not fear any private demands for payment or gratuity from me for any service whatsoever. Where pleasure is both given and taken, there can be no thought of payment.''

Five

The full moon freed itself from the branches of a palm and sailed up into a black sky while Caroline stood watching it, trembling with the seductive memory of Kaifar's eyes as he had offered her his body and his passion. Of the jolt of electric desire that had coursed through her at his suggestion, that was now again making her both weak and strong.

"Please don't talk to me like this," she had said, with a feeble attempt at firmness in her voice that she could only pray had fooled him. "I have not come to your country in search of a holiday fling."

"There is a word in your language for finding a treasure that one did not seek, I think."

Against a backdrop of rhythmical wailing from the old woman, Caroline looked away from Kaifar's disturbing gaze. "There is a word in my language for what you are doing, too. Sexual harassment," she returned.

His laughter was free and effortless. "Caroline, we have a bond, you and I. You have felt it, too."

She had no answer.

"How old is your fiancé?" he whispered. "The man I spoke to did not have the voice of a young man." She made no reply. "A woman with your passions should not be tied to one whose passions are already faded.

"Caroline," he breathed, close to her ear so that she could hear every drawled syllable of her name in spite of the singer, though she should have drawn back. Distantly she wondered when he had begun to use her first name. "I can give you memories to warm the long, cold nights you will suffer in the bed of this old man."

"Kaifar, I am engaged."

All she had to do to break the spell he was casting on her was sit back, but she felt bound to him, bound to his words and his voice as the source of her lifeblood. "What would I take from him that is of value to him? How do you rob him by giving to me what he will not want?"

She did sit back. "What he will want from me is loyalty," she said. "And he is entitled to that."

Kaifar had only nodded, accepting her decision, and then immediately applied himself to the delicious food. After a moment Caroline had done the same.

Now, under the moon, she lifted her hands and drew the hot curls from her neck, allowing the soft wind to blow through them. Kaifar was right. He had a passion that neither David nor her father nor any of their cohorts had. Age had nothing to do with it; it was a way of being. Not mere sexual passion, though she was in no doubt he had that. The passion for living, for experiencing...what? Love, life, truth? *Everything.*

She believed, though the thought was hardly coherent, that his own strong passions were what made him comfortable with hers. For the first time in her life, Caroline's emotions did not frighten a man. For the first time, she did not feel from a man the slightly panicked urge to stifle her feeling nature, to make it neater, more comfortable...to control her.

David was very practised in the way he controlled her, the fire within her, with a combination of disapproval, distaste, and outright command. She had no armour against him. He would win the battle. He would stifle her.

Kaifar, on the other hand—she shuddered. If she let him—if she even relaxed her guard—Kaifar would pour gasoline on her fires, and then would lead her, safely or not, through the inferno of her own burning. She shivered as the thought and the desire that arose in its wake pulsed through her. Even thinking about him ignited her. What if he touched her? What defence would she have?

"Today," Kaifar said, "I will show you the Great Mosque."

Ignoring the high-handed manner of the invitation, since she really wanted to see the mosque, Caroline only asked mildly, "Is what I'm wearing okay?"

She was wearing a white flowing jersey cotton summer dress, calf-length, its neckline, sleeves, waist and hem banded with alternate bands of navy and green, and navy sandals on bare feet. Kaifar's eyes obediently moved over her, and she felt the look like a little electric shock. He affected her on every level—her pulses raced, her heart ached, her soul yearned, her spirit leapt at the unfamiliarly intimate mental touch. Her family was not noted for its closeness; maybe that was why she had been willing to accept so little from David—she had learned to accept that there was no more than that. But one day in Kaifar's company had showed her a different truth.

Caroline surfaced to the sound of Kaifar's voice. "This is very attractive. They will offer you *hejab*—what do you call head covering?—scarf!" he answered himself. "Are you willing to cover your head in the mosque?"

"Yes, of course," she said mildly. "I'll bring my own." She ran up to her room and returned in a few minutes with the gauzy green scarf she had worn last night draped over her arm. Kaifar nodded approval.

"Some Western women object to this request," he observed later, in the car.

She stared. "Do you mean people would rather not go inside that beautiful building than put a scarf on?"

"It is a house of God. We do not turn away people who do not respect the dress codes, but there is no doubt that such people often offend those who worship in the mosque."

"I wonder how they'd feel if someone from Barakat lit a cigarette in a no-smoking building in New York."

Kaifar laughed as if charmed by her original thinking. "Perhaps we should put up signs to this effect."

There was something in the way he said it that made Caroline glance curiously at him. "Do you mean you actually have some responsibility for the mosque?"

"Every citizen has such responsibility."

"Do they all feel it as strongly as you?"

He paused to negotiate around a mule and its cartload of melons. "My father was Guardian of the National Treasures during his lifetime. He raised us with a devotion to the nation."

She wondered what tragedy had occurred to make the son of such an important man a mere tour guide. It certainly accounted for a lot of what seemed contradictory in him. Perhaps it even accounted for some of the fellow feeling she had for Kaifar—had his family, too, suffered a fall from grace? "When did he die?"

"Eleven years ago, peace be upon his name."

"Is your mother alive?"

"My mother, yes. She was younger than my father, she is in good health."

"Where does she live?"

He watched her in the mirror as he pulled up at a light. "My mother lives in my house, that was my father's. Your parents live with you, also?"

"I live with them." Suddenly she found herself telling him about her family's disaster. She wasn't sure whether he would understand what she said about the stock market, but he asked no questions. "The house was just about the only thing my father didn't lose, because it's been in his family for years and the title was tied up in a peculiar way. But without my salary they couldn't stay there."

To her surprise, Kaifar frowned. "Do you tell me that your parents still live in a large house suitable to a man with extensive wealth, after being financially ruined? And that your salary is what allows this? That you have given up your education so that your father and mother should not have to face the fact of their lives?"

He sounded amazed, almost angry. She thought suddenly that she would not want him as an enemy. He would be dangerous, implacable. Ruthless. "When you put it that way, it sounds ridiculous."

"Worse than ridiculous. You have an obligation to your parents, but that they should use you in this way is unjust when the alternative is not starvation, nor even hunger, merely a lifestyle in keeping with their reduced income."

In typical human response, she began to defend them. "They didn't demand," she said, blinding herself for the moment to the much greater sacrifice they had demanded from her. "And if they moved, they'd lose all their friends. They've lived there all their lives."

"Their friends would not visit them in another neighbourhood? What kind of friends can these be?"

Caroline half smiled and shook her head. How to make him understand the society that her parents were part of, were so desperate to go on being part of? "You don't understand."

Her voice was calm, but she felt shaken. What would his opinion be if he knew all the truth—that she was being married off to David to put the family fortunes right once and for all?

Somehow she had imagined that his opinions would be different. That as someone from an older society, less individualistic, less concerned with women's rights, more respectful of age, he would have approved the sacrifice of a daughter to her father's hopes.

Almost as if reading her thoughts, he said, "I understand that a man must be a man!"

She had no answer for that, and there was silence for a few minutes as Kaifar steered the car through the diverse morning traffic. They were obviously near a large market: people were carrying a huge variety of produce and wares in ancient trucks, overladen bicycles, carts, suitcases, bags, on their backs and on the backs of mules. Caroline watched, fascinated by the colour and noise, as they passed.

Then Kaifar roused her by speaking again. "What work do you do?" he asked.

"I'm a saleswoman in a designer boutique," she told him. It was not the job she would have chosen, but as it turned out she was good at it. With commission she made a better income than ordinary office work could have given her. And, being slim, she got some great clothes at ridiculous prices. "Some of my old friends are customers." It was a fact that they enjoyed more than she did.

"Your father lost his money, but you did not lose your beauty," Kaifar said cryptically.

Caroline sighed unconsciously. It was a relief to talk to Kaifar. No doubt some people would say it was because he was a stranger, that it was a ships-that-pass-in-the-night thing, but she didn't think so. Maybe it was even the opposite: because he did not feel like a stranger to her. He felt like someone she had been waiting to meet. But that was a dangerous thought, and it was banished before it was fully formed.

As a dilapidated bicycle laden with wrapped packages and an old man in a keffiyeh teetered precariously in the car's path, Kaifar expertly braked.

"*Ya Allah!*" cried the old man, recognizing the danger now that it was past, then wobbling on his way.

"Could we visit the market later?" Caroline asked.

Kaifar flicked a glance over his shoulder at her, then urged the car forward again. "You have purchases you wish to make?"

"I don't know that till I see what's on offer." She hadn't experienced the bustling excitement of a street market since one of the happiest times of her life: a visit to Italy when she was thirteen. She had gotten drunk on the sensual impact of colour, sound, smell, and human community, and her father's disapproval had had less impact where there had been so much moral support. Ever since then she had felt that buying vegetables in a supermarket was a deprivation, if not a sin.

She was not sure how she knew that he was reluctant to take her to the market. When he made no answer, she let the subject slide. There was no reason for her not to go on her own one day.

A discreet sign in several Western languages in the court-yard of the fabulous, breathtakingly beautiful mosque announced, "You are entering a sacred place where the devout may be worshipping at any time. Please observe our customs. Men and women should be decorously dressed. Women are asked to cover their hair. Squares of cloth are provided inside the main entrance."

Nearby sat an ancient beggar, cross-legged, a white turban twisted around his white hair, a long beard curling down his chest, his eyes bright. A dirty embroidered cap on the ground in front of him showed the scant proceeds of his morning's work. Kaifar stopped and bent over, his hand outstretched. *"Salaam aleikum,"* he said.

The beggar reached his gnarled hand up with a nod of thanks; then his grip on Kaifar's hand tightened, and he bent forward to kiss it. *"Waleikum salaam, Sayedi,"* he replied formally. He let go of Kaifar's hand, and looked first at the banknote that had changed hands and then back at Kaifar. Grinning, he stroked his beard and said something to which Kaifar replied with a laugh and a comment. The old beggar laughed uproariously and slipped the note into his robe.

"Do you always give to beggars?" she asked, as they moved on. She thought of David, refusing even to buy a charity raffle ticket. He had told her he never gave money to beggars. *They've all got condominiums, Caroline. Don't be taken in.*

Kaifar only smiled down at her as if the question were ridiculous. "Charity is one of the Pillars of Islam. Did not Jesus also require this of his followers?"

"Aren't you worried that they're not legitimate?"

"Legitimate?"

"Maybe they aren't really needy, you know. Maybe it's just an easy way to earn a living."

"Does your country then have no people who are truly poor?"

She felt heat in her cheeks and wanted to disown the sentiment as David's. "Yes, of course it has."

"There are many poor people in Barakat. But even if this case were as you describe it, Caroline, if he were not truly needy, that would be a problem for him, not for me."

"It would?" she asked with a quizzical smile.

Kaifar said, as if it were self-evident, "It is between him and God. My instructions are to give to beggars, not to inquire into their hearts."

Caroline glanced down at her flashing diamond solitaire. *I did not accept David because of his religion or character or morals,* she reminded herself brutally. *I accepted him because he was rich.*

Inside the ornately carved doors of the mosque, a small, dark, smiling woman made as if to approach Caroline with a plastic bag filled with scarves, but withdrew as Caroline shook out her scarf, folded it into a triangle and draped it over her head.

He was a fascinating guide, informed and articulate. David was also informed about his subject; Caroline by now had plenty of experience of following a man around and listening to him expound about what she was seeing. But either David's manner was at fault, or Caroline's natural interest was sparked by Barakat much more than by Classical Greece and Rome. As Kaifar described Queen Halimah's great deeds among her people—she had built bridges and roads and hospitals as well as mosques—Caroline was entranced. As he talked about the craftsmen employed in the building of the mosque, she shook her head in wonder at their astonishing art. And as she gazed up at lofty mirrored domes and gold leaf calligraphy and mosaic patterns almost too beautifully intricate to take in, she sighed and wished that Western buildings could be a quarter as beautiful, or give a tenth of this lift to the spirits. That was not the only thing that she wished in that sacred place, but some of her wishes were hidden from her own heart.

Kaifar did not lecture her the way David did—as though, finding her unsatisfactory, he was hell-bent on educating her. Kaifar told her stories, he shared secrets with her, he made her laugh, and sigh, and open her eyes with astonishment. Without realizing it, Caroline began to lean into his strong shoulder as she listened and moved through the mosque beside him, as though the protection of that shoulder were her right. When they had finished the tour, Caroline felt mentally fresh, as she might after a bath in spring water.

The call to prayer of the muezzin began over their heads as they strolled side by side through the square. *Allahu akhbar, Allahu akhbar...*

She felt more at peace now than she could remember feeling for years. Everything seemed right. It was as if some question she had asked had been answered, but she did not know what question, and had not yet heard the answer.

Kaifar led her back to the limousine and opened the door for her. For a moment before starting the engine, he sat looking at her. She met his eyes, but could not hold the piercing gaze. He opened his mouth and she thought he was going to say something, but all he asked was "Lunch?" just as Caroline broke the gaze and turned self-consciously away.

The nervous turning of her head brought a vehicle on an adjacent side of the square into her line of vision. It was a nondescript white van, indistinguishable from dozens of others that one saw in any city. But she noticed idly that as Kaifar passed the spot where it was parked, the white van made a U-turn and pulled into traffic behind them.

* * *

"This is the Bostan al Sa'adat—The Garden of Joy. Here we can eat lunch and afterwards stroll through the various gardens," Kaifar said. Caroline was glad there was no need to do more than nod her assent. She was open-mouthed and speechless with what she saw: inside a high wall that enclosed several acres, there were fountains, rivers, canals, pavilions, follies, gazebos, and every kind of plant and tree and bird imaginable. Animals roamed amongst the plants and waterways, and even among the people.

This garden, he told her, had been endowed for all the people by Sheikh Daud, the last king of Barakat, sixty years ago, upon the occasion of his marriage to the beautiful foreigner for whose sake he promised to take no other wife so long as she lived. It had taken twenty years to complete.

Caroline blinked. "But I thought Sheikh Daud had three sons by three different wives, and wanted them all to inherit equally, and that was why the kingdom was broken up into three emirates. Aren't they under some command never to raise a weapon to their brothers or their brothers' descendants on pain of some dreadful curse?"

"This is true, but what is missing from your story is the great love story of Sheikh Daud and the woman to whom he gave the name Azizah. She promised to marry him only if he would swear never to take another bride, but when their two sons were both killed in the same accident, Queen Azizah released him from his promise. The king married three new brides in a single day."

"Sounds like a recipe for disaster," Caroline said lightly, and Kaifar grinned.

"There were many stories of harem intrigues, with each mother putting forward her son as the only possible heir to the throne, but the old sheikh managed it very— Look at this, Caroline!" he commanded suddenly, drawing her off the flagstone path and along a narrow dirt path winding through trees.

As she followed him, Caroline's attention was briefly on an important-looking group of men who had just entered the main path ahead of them. They all looked like the Middle Eastern potentates she was always seeing on the evening news. Nothing was really remarkable about them— except that she had the strange feeling that Kaifar had turned off the path in order to avoid them.

For a moment she pondered this, and Kaifar's earlier unexpressed but clear reluctance to take her to the market. Perhaps he did not like having old friends see him in his work? For the son of a man who had once held such a post as Guardian of the National Treasures...Caroline understood how cruel former friends could be, even when they didn't intend to be.

But he led her to a picturesque, very old stone bridge, which was certainly worth seeing, that spanned a stream too narrow to require it. They stood in the middle, leaning on the parapet, looking down at the flowing water.

"This bridge also was built by Queen Halimah," he said. "The gardens were built just here for that reason."

"Why did she build a long bridge over a tiny stream?"

Kaifar smiled. "The geography of the area has changed since the bridge was built. This was once a major tributary of the Sa'adat River, and since the nearest ford was many miles away the bridge was a boon for which the people were extremely grateful. There are the ruins of bridges even in the middle of the desert, proving that the course of the River Sa'adat itself has changed."

Caroline nodded. They stood in silence, absorbing the peace and the perfume of the many flowers. He was on her left, and it was a simple matter for him to take her left hand and examine the massive diamond solitaire.

"Your fiancé is a very rich man?"

She nodded. "Very."

"How does your fiancé feel about the role you play in your parents' life?"

Caroline moved restlessly. "I don't think David's ever thought about it."

"He, of course, will take you away from that life. Does he pay your father a large dowry for you?"

Caroline snatched her hand back. "Dowry? Don't be ridiculous!" she laughed. "We don't have dowries in the States! Women aren't bought and sold like cattle the way they are in the East!"

He stood looking impassively down at her. "Aren't you, Caroline?"

And with a terrible clarity, she saw it. *But that's just what it is. David is paying Dad a huge sum for me, and that's the formal term for an exchange like that, isn't it? Dowry. I'm being sold, like any Third World bride.*

Six

Sitting close to Kaifar that evening at an intimate, low table loaded with yet more succulent and sensual food, lying against silk carpets and brocaded cushions, she could no longer ignore the fact that he was a devastatingly attractive, sensual and sexual man.

She didn't really understand what kind of place this was; it hardly seemed like a restaurant. He had stopped the car in a dark, narrow side street beside a high wall. He had got out of the car, leaving it running, and out of the darkness a man had appeared to drive the car away. He led her to an unlighted door in the wall which she had not seen, opened it, and led her through the darkness of a beautiful garden to a low table and chairs set among flowering shrubs. She could hear running water, as if a fountain were near, and smell flowers.

There, by an impassive man in white *shalwar kamees*, they had been served with a drink and a plate of tasty morsels before Kaifar led her inside to one of the most beautiful rooms Caroline had ever seen. Arched windows and doorways in rich dark wood against white painted walls, a domed ceiling of beautiful stained glass, silk carpets, cushions, low tables, plants, jars, paintings, and perfectly placed lamps combined to produce an utterly sensual air of beauty and comfort on a level she couldn't recall ever having experienced.

There was one attentive waiter, and the Eastern equivalent of a maitre d', but there were only two or three tables in the room and she couldn't see or hear any other diners in the other rooms that seemed to lead off through half a dozen doorways and arches off the corridor.

"Where are we, Kaifar?" she whispered once.

"Pardon me?"

"I can't believe we have the place to ourselves! Why aren't there more customers?"

"People eat late in Barakat," Kaifar said, smiling into her eyes so that she forgot what her question had been.

His fingers touched her lips as he masterfully placed a succulent morsel between them, and Caroline felt her heart thud with a mixture of desire and anticipation more delicious, if possible, than the food.

He made it impossible to resist. An almost matter-of-fact attitude disguised his deeply sensual intent. "Ah, you must taste this, Caroline!" he said, and reached for a plate the waiter was just setting down. He lifted something on his fork and fed her like a child, one hand lightly under her chin, the other sliding the fork into her helplessly open mouth.

Garlic, spices, oil, the soft tender flesh of some vegetable she did not recognize, and Kaifar's eyes smiling at her with masculine approval, all these created a delicious taste on her hungry tongue and in her hungry heart, and as he caught an errant drop of the spicy oil with his finger from her lower lip and brushed it between her lips so that her tongue involuntarily licked it, she was assailed by a kick of lust that left her breathless.

This was seduction. In spite of his subtlety she knew this was deliberate seduction. And yet she could not resist the power of it. It was too potent, more powerful than anything she had experienced before. "Your customers must fall like leaves in autumn," she observed with a helpless shake of her head.

"Never with such hunger," he murmured, as if the mental, physical and sensual need she knew she was betraying with every movement and every word was itself delicious to him.

He had shaved his beard off, revealing the strength of his chin and jaw, and that, too, affected her senses.

She looked at the huge diamond on her finger. In this light it did not sparkle, it seemed dull. As dull as her feelings for her fiancé. "I'm an engaged woman," she muttered, more for her benefit than his. Kaifar did not respond; only carefully chose and lifted a small, succulently spiced meatball in his fingers and offered it to her mouth.

Tonight Caroline was wearing a favourite dress, maroon raw silk with long sleeves, high to the neck in front but deeply V-necked at the back, leaving her naked to the waist, a full skirt springing from a waist set low on her hips. It was one that she had been given by her employer because in it she was a walking advertisement for the boutique. Tonight her hair, her golden curls tousled over her head and neck, was adorned by the one thing David had given her that she liked—a golden band that encircled her brow, with a large square-cut ruby in the middle of her forehead.

From in front she looked like a medieval painting of the

virgin, from behind like a wanton. David had never liked the dress, but if the appreciation in his eyes was her marker, Kaifar did.

She drank two glasses of wine before she felt his hand on her naked back. It was the lightest of touches, but her body had been waiting for it. Her skin leapt, her blood burned. She understood, by the deep and throbbing response of both body and soul to him now, that she had been attracted to Kaifar from the very first moment of laying eyes on him, that the root of why it had been so easy for him to unsettle her was this: that she was more drawn to him than she could ever remember feeling in her life.

Dimly she remembered a story from her childhood, about a knight who put his sword on the bed between himself and a girl he was protecting, so that he would not make love to her during the night. Caroline looked at the diamond ring that was the symbol of her promise to her parents and to David, and knew that she could not allow Kaifar to do what it was clearly his intention to do tonight. He must not be allowed to make love to her, not even if that lovemaking would be the sexual high point of all her life, past and future, not even if it were her once-in-a-lifetime chance for the kind of fulfilment most women dreamed of.

"No more wine, thank you," she said when the waiter next picked up the flask.

Kaifar made no protest, merely quirked an eyebrow at the waiter, who set the flask down again. Another course of food arrived, grilled meats and spicy potatoes, all sending up an aroma as seductive to the culinary senses as Kaifar was to her sexual receptors. Caroline laughed weakly. She felt assailed from all sides, but she couldn't refuse to eat!

"Why do you laugh, my pearl past price? What amuses you?"

His voice was rough, threaded with the impatience of a man who wants what he wants. That "pearl past price" would have sounded ridiculous on any other man's tongue, but on his it was just more magic. Caroline shook her head to clear it, a movement that set tendrils of her hair in motion over the bare sensitive skin just at the junction of neck and back, sending little messages of pleasure and promise down the skin of her arms and breasts.

She opted for challenge. "Kaifar, do you seduce all your women clients like this?"

"Do I seduce you?" he countered, looking lazily up at her through his lashes from where he lay on one elbow against the pillows.

"You know that you do!"

"Good," he said. His hand came up and drew on a curl of her hair, so that the end wrapped around his forefinger, clinging gold against teak. Pulling her gently down, and bending close, he brushed his mouth against her neck, then lifted his head to gaze into her eyes. "See how this curl cleaves to my finger," he observed. "Your being and mine on every level are like this."

"You haven't answered my question," Caroline insisted, clinging to her sanity like a mast in a hurricane.

He released the lock of hair, watching as Caroline rubbed her neck to reduce the electric tension his touch had produced on her skin. "I have never had a single woman client before, so there is no answer. Maybe after you I will be addicted to such pleasures. Maybe I will seduce all that come in my way. Or perhaps—" his voice dropped to a husky whisper "—no other woman will ever do for me again, Caroline, only you. What then?"

She felt it stab her heart. God, could he be telling her the truth? Were they falling in love? Was that what was happening? Or was it only her?

Was she falling in love with Kaifar? Her heart thudded at the thought. If what was shaking her up so unbelievably was merely lust, it was bad enough—maybe she had needed an encounter like this to show her how impossible marriage to David Percy would be. But if it was *love*—and if he also felt it—what would she do? What could they do?

Tonight he was dressed in black—a polo-necked shirt that revealed his powerfully muscled chest and arms, and front-pleated pants worn with a black leather belt and a curiously wrought silver buckle that showed off his slim waist and flat stomach. He looked as perfectly proportioned as a Greek god—*or a polo player!* she mentally amended, thinking, *It's as though someone researched my deepest fantasies and produced him out of a hat!*

In an uncharacteristic burst of paranoia, she wondered if perhaps this whole thing—the raffle, her win, the exotic locale, and a man as handsome as a prince out of *The Arabian Nights*—had been concocted for a purpose.

Even the white vans that seemed to be always around were explained by this interpretation of events—maybe they were taking pictures of such intimacies as this meal, with Kaifar holding out tender delicacies to her, and her finding it impossible to turn away.

But for whom? Who could have such a purpose? Her father had always said she had too much imagination for one person. Who could possibly have an interest in her breaking her engagement?

David, something in her whispered. Caroline gasped faintly. Suppose David himself had changed his mind, and now regretted his bargain? She had not read the pre-nuptial agreement, she had just not wanted to know what price had been put on her. Suppose there was a financial cost for his breaking the engagement? Suppose further that if Caroline were caught in another man's bed that cost was waived? That might give him a motive for making the fault hers.

Maybe it was David who was paying for the first-class treatment, David who had paid for Kaifar's time. That might even account for Kaifar's strange reaction to David on the phone—overdoing it because David wasn't a stranger to him.

Suddenly Caroline laughed at her own restless paranoia. Kaifar certainly unsettled her. She would be doubting her own name next!

Kaifar smiled and slipped food into his own mouth with sensual enjoyment. "What has made you laugh, Durri?"

She tilted her head, smiling down where he lay at her shoulder. It was really too intimate, this manner of eating, it was almost as if they were in bed together. "What does Durri mean?"

He dropped his head back, piercing her with a look of fierce possessiveness so that she lost her breath. "My pearl," he translated. "Tell me, my pearl, what has made you laugh?"

She said, "I was just wondering, in my paranoid way, if David hired you to try to break our engagement."

His warm eyes turned into two splinters of chipped glass, hard and cruel. "Hired me? David Percy?" He sounded just the way he had when she'd suggested David could have bought the Great Mosque of Halimah. Furiously insulted.

She shivered. "Sorry, Kaifar, I didn't mean to offend you. It was just a little paranoid fantasy I was entertaining." His anger always made her nervous. It was something almost primitive, like her nervous fear of thunderstorms. And sometimes he did seem like a force of nature.

His eyes lost their anger and he picked up a green olive, tossing it into his mouth. "I did not know that your fiancé wanted to break your engagement. Is this, then, why he did not come with you?"

He spoke lightly, but there was still something behind the words which made her nervous. Would he take advantage if he thought David had changed his mind, or would he lose interest because she was not someone else's property?

"No, that's why I was laughing at myself," she explained feebly. She sounded like a fool and knew it. "It's because you're—I mean, if someone had picked you out of a catalogue according to all the things that I most—" Suddenly seeing what kind of confession she was about to make, Caroline choked, coloured, and reached out blindly to a plate, putting something delicious at random into her mouth.

Kaifar leaned towards her, intrigued. "According to all the things that you most—?" he prodded.

"I forgot what I was going to say," Caroline muttered, chewing hard. "My, this is delicious! What on earth is it?"

He caught her hand as she reached for another delicacy, drawing her around to face him, his other hand enclosing her chin and forcing her to look down at him where he lay. Her eyes were almost black, the pupils enlarged like a startled cat's. For a moment they were caught, a man and a woman snared in the tangle of feeling that was between them. Just for a split second the world held its breath, as though she must lean down to kiss him, and his arms must go around her, and they must make love.

"According to all the things you most—?" he insisted after that moment of full silence.

She dropped her lashes down over her eyes, to hide from him, because she was sure he could read whatever was there.

"Look at me," he commanded. He waited, and she was compelled to obey.

"I am not what you dream of, Caroline," he said ruthlessly. "Do not dream of me, for you know nothing of what I am. This—" he stroked her lower lip with a long finger "this I can give you, and I will. But look no further than the pleasure my body will give you. I will give you something to remember during the cold nights when you lie beside your husband, Caroline. And like a squirrel you must store up the memories for the long winter ahead."

Tears started in her eyes, and with an exclamation she slapped his hand away from her face. What a fool she was! What had she been imagining? She should consider herself lucky he had spelled it out for her; probably thousands of his countrymen would not! Her eyes burned, and she bit her lip, the sharp little pain acting as a backfire to the firestorm that threatened within. She would not let him see how much dreaming she had done without knowing it, nor how much his words hurt her.

She turned and smiled down at him. "I'm afraid you seriously underestimate David's sexual abilities," said Caroline.

Seven

Silence fell again. His eyes looked very dark, and although on the surface his expression did not alter, something seemed to shift inside as they gazed at each other.

"You find him a satisfactory lover?" Kaifar said, through shut teeth.

She didn't find him a lover at all. Her entire experience of David's lovemaking was one kiss, and the promise, "You will find that I carry out my marital duties quite enthusiastically when the time comes, Caroline," in a tone which had raised a chill in her soul.

But she wasn't going to admit that to Kaifar, not after what he had just said. "Older men do have experience on their side," she pointed out with a smug smile.

"So do younger men," Kaifar said softly. "The experience of when a woman is lying."

He was jealous! He did not want to think of her in David's bed! She looked challengingly down at him, not replying, glorying in the knowledge, even while she knew she had no right. His feelings were stronger than he wanted to admit.

They were alone in the room now, both the staff having disappeared into another room. In a fury, Kaifar lifted her hand and pressed his mouth into the palm, passionately kissing it, his mouth open, again and again, as if he meant to eat her, the heat and damp of his lips trailing blood and fire—his fire, her blood, as if her veins themselves were drawn by the magnetism of his mouth.

It was completely unexpected, such a passionate assault on her senses that Caroline could not suppress the cry that came to her throat, the wild shiver of desire that made her whole body electric. He heard it, felt it in her, and looked up from behind her hand, still pressed to his mouth, with a dark, possessive triumph in his eyes that almost felled her.

"Perhaps it is some time since you enjoyed his attentions," he suggested. And then he released her captive hand and slowly, ruthlessly, pulled her down into his strong arms, his passionate embrace.

A breath of astonishment escaped her as her chest met his, but then his hand moved to cup her head and the sigh was drowned in his kiss. A kiss that teased, tasted, drank, and was nectar on her lips. Her body shivered with joy and pleasure, and whispered that this touch was as inevitable as death, as necessary as life, and her only reason for being born.

His fingers stroked her back from her neck all down her spine to just below her waist, skin on skin, sending rivulets of hot sensation through her, so that for a brief moment of unreality her shocked brain told her that he had undressed her, and responded wildly. She gasped with mingled shock and pleasure, then laughed as she remembered what dress she wore.

Kaifar laughed, too, his dark eyes glinting up into hers, and lifted his head to kiss her throat under her ear. Then his smile faded. "Give me your mouth," he ordered.

A glass on the table beside them rattled, and Caroline turned her head, suddenly reminded of where they were. "Kaifar, the waiter!" she whispered.

"Can you think of the waiter at such a time? Give me your mouth," he whispered insistently.

But reality had intruded and would not be banished. She could not allow him to make love to her in a public place—she could not allow him to make love to her at all.

"No," she said, struggling out of his arms.

He did not understand. He smiled and rose smoothly to his feet, put down a hand and drew her up after. "Come with me."

His hand around her waist guided her firmly through the beautiful room and down a corridor to an ancient wooden door under a curving arch. The door opened silently under his hand. Before Caroline had time to draw breath, she was standing in a massive room, softly lighted, beautifully decorated, where a luxurious bed strewn with pillows had been turned down for the night.

She stared around her in shock. What kind of a restaurant was this? Where had this come from?

"Where are the others?" she demanded stupidly, trying to force her brain to work.

"They have gone," he assured her. "They will not return."

She experienced a little jolt. "How do you know? What kind of place is this?"

"Very discreet," he said. His hand stroked her back so that she shivered, and he slowly drew her into his embrace.

She could feel his body stir against her, and something in her gloried in her own sexual power.

But from somewhere—perhaps her nervous doubts as to what kind of place she was in, she got the strength to pull out of his embrace. "I have a fiancé, Kaifar."

He let her go, but reached up and touched a curl of her hair, which of its own accord wrapped itself around his strong forefinger again, reminding her of what he had said. They stood there, not quite touching, while her body yearned for his.

"He has purchased you with wealth. I offer pleasure, Caroline. A night, a week of lovemaking with me, for the pleasure it gives us both."

The cynicism of it chilled the consuming heat of her desire for him. She was half glad, half sorry. She stood further away from him and, without looking at him, said bitterly, "He has purchased me, as you put it, with the promise of happiness and security for my family."

"Why do you make such a sacrifice for those who do not love you?"

She gasped with shock as his words, finding no resistance in her, pierced straight to her soul. She glared at him. "They do love me! How do you know they don't love me? You don't know my parents."

Kaifar shook his head. "One who loves does not ask for the total sacrifice of the loved one, Caroline."

She dropped her head into her hands, covering her face. "Stop it!" she ordered furiously. "Just stop this, please!"

"You know it is true."

She did know it was true. She had always known it. The truth was not that she made the sacrifice because her parents loved her, but because they did not. Because, in some small, childish part of her, she was still hoping that if she were "good" she would win their love. In her newly vulnerable state, she could not hide from the truth.

He was quick to press his advantage. "By the rules you have made for yourself, Caroline, what do you get from this—deal?" He emphasised the word, his rough voice brushing away the gilt on the arrangement between David and her father to reveal the base metal underneath.

He must not be allowed to undermine her like this. She had to protect herself. Caroline stiffened, and smiled. "A very nice lifestyle," she said. "Richer than you could possibly imagine."

He was not daunted. It was almost as if this was the answer he had expected to hear. "And for this you sell not only yourself but also all your hope of pleasure, too? Why? What will your fiancé gain from your rejection of the pleasure we could share?"

"Leave me alone!" she cried with a sudden burst of feeling that surprised her, as if the lie she had just told was making her ill. "How dare you do this to me, for the sake of a week's sex? I wish I had listened to my mother! Oh, God, why did I ever come here?"

"You know why you came," he pursued ruthlessly. "You came for a last taste of freedom, Caroline. That taste is what I offer you. Why do you not take it?"

The condemned man ate a hearty meal, she heard herself say. And with a hollow, sinking heart, she thought, *He's right. Without even knowing it, that's why I came. I'm a hypocrite, secretly planning to eat my cake while I have it.*

The tears dried on her cheeks and she stood straight and firm. "Please take me back to the hotel," she said.

His eyes flared with a feeling she couldn't name. "Caroline," he whispered.

She gazed at him. "No," was all she said.

* * *

Kaifar opened the door to the hotel and watched as Caroline passed in.

"Good night," she said.

He nodded and watched as she crossed to the elevators. A man crossing the lobby stopped and pushed the button again. When the elevator came, he followed her inside.

Kaifar turned and went down the steps to the car. Slipping into the driver's seat, he reached across to the glove compartment, pulled out a phone and dialled. After a few moments, a voice answered in English with "Where are you?"

"Outside the hotel."

"Outside the *hotel?*"

"It did not go well."

"What? I got a call saying you were 'getting on like a house affair'!"

Kaifar laughed, then sobered. "That changed suddenly. My mistake."

"Why the hell didn't you just snatch her? Why take her—" There was the sound of a frustrated breath.

"It would have frightened her," said Kaifar.

"It's got to be done. Everything is already in progress."

"Tomorrow," Kaifar promised, and hung up.

Caroline wandered up and down in her hotel suite, trying to make sense of things. It was a journey of a thousand miles, and she could not seem to take a single step of rational thought. Only one thing was clear—she would not drift into a sexual liaison with Kaifar and then go home to marry David. Either she was engaged and owed him her loyalty, or she was a free woman. She would not sell her self-respect, whatever else she sold.

But that left the bigger question: could she go through with it? *Should* she marry David?

One who loves does not ask for the total sacrifice of the loved one. He had said that tonight, and it was true.

Deep inside, it was not a new idea to Caroline, the thought that her parents did not love her. As a young child she had felt it as a daily truth. They had not cherished her, what she was, her talents, her peculiarities, least of all her capacity to feel deeply. They had only tried, without much success, to mould her into something they *could* love.

They had loved her brother Thom almost to the point of worship, they had cherished Dara as the pretty baby, but Caroline they had tolerated, pretending to love her when it suited them.

She thought of how her approval rating had soared once she had agreed to this contract of marriage with a cold-hearted, cold-blooded, selfish man twice her age. A man whose physical presence chilled her like the touch of death. Suddenly she had become the golden-haired girl. She thought of the pride with which her father now introduced her as ''my little girl who happened to catch David Percy's eye.'' Before that she had been ''my daughter Caroline.'' ''My son Thom, who's sailing through university''; ''My son the financial wizard of the family.'' She had heard those often enough. And even Dara came in for a share of pride and affection. ''Our baby, Dara.''

Caroline had been the cuckoo in the nest. Her father had said to her mother once, in her hearing, after Caroline had displeased him with a public display of emotion, ''You were holidaying alone the year before Caroline was born—Greece, wasn't it? I suppose you didn't meet a swan?''

Caroline had not understood the allusion, she had imagined it had something to do with some superstition about pregnant women being frightened by various things and producing monsters. It was a few years before she came across the story of Leda, the maiden seduced by the god Zeus disguised as a swan.

Perhaps that was why he had never loved her. Because he suspected, or knew, that she was not his. One day, when she was about fifteen, she had asked her mother, "Who is my real father?" and had received a slap across the mouth whose mark had lingered for hours.

She had forgotten about it after that. But now her mind was a whirl of things forgotten, suppressed, ignored...she was being assaulted by the truth of her situation. Everything that as a child, for the sake of self-preservation, she had suppressed and forgotten, was alive now.

She tried to telephone home, but there was a problem with the lines. She wanted to talk to her mother. Every five minutes she changed her mind about everything.

Kaifar's refusal to take any responsibility for her future was the final shock. It forced her to face the reality of her choices. There were only two options—marry David Percy, or break off the engagement. It was not a choice between David and a man she was deeply drawn to but scarcely knew, between country club living and a foreign lifestyle she could barely comprehend. It was David, or no one. David or independence. David or telling her father he had made his bed and the time had come for all of them to lie in it.

David or her life.

Even in those terms it was not an easy choice. Or at least, not all the time. Caroline felt herself wavering from decision to indecision, from belief to uncertainty, from confidence to the deeply buried, newly rediscovered sense of her own unworthiness that had secretly haunted her life.

If only she could have phoned during her moments of clarity and told David it was over! If only she could have talked to her mother and father, told them what she meant to do! But every time she picked up the receiver she was met with the same fatalistic indifference and the information that the lines were being fixed.

She was left to make her decision over and over again, and doubt it over and over again.

She felt so close to Kaifar it seemed impossible he could feel nothing but sexual desire for her. With half of her mind she believed that he was lying, if not to her, then to himself, when he told her there was no future for them, only a week of sex. "The gentleman protests too much, methinks," she muttered to herself as she paced the night out, but then she doubted that, too. Kaifar was not the kind of man who did not know his own mind, was he? He wanted her sexually but in no other way. She must be very clear about that. There was no magical new future far away from the repercussions of her actions if she broke the engagement. She would be going home to face the music.

Caroline picked up the phone again. "Please, I want to call New York!" she cried. "When will the lines be clear?"

"I do not know, Madame. But it is very late now."

"What does that mean? Does that mean no one is trying to fix the lines?"

"The engineer has gone home, Madame."

"*Engineer?* I thought it was a problem with the lines out of the country!"

There was a pause. "The problem is with the hotel lines to the international operator!" said the receptionist, as if he had pulled a rabbit out of a very difficult linguistic hat.

All this time she had believed it was a problem beyond the hotel's control! If she had known a few hours ago she could have found another phone! Suddenly all Caroline's distress had an outlet. "Gone home! Haven't you got an emergency engineer?'' she shouted with all the pent-up frustration of the past few miserable hours.

"But it is not an emergency, Madame. Only, the lines are not working. They will be fixed tomorrow, perhaps.''

"You wouldn't know an emergency if it bit you!'' she exploded, but it got her nowhere against the practised fatalism of the receptionist.

In the early hours, tired, frustrated, and depressed, Caroline began to fear herself. She would be weak. If she could not take some irrevocable step now, she might never again have the courage.

Under the power of that fear she sat down and wrote instead. She would get it on paper, she would stamp and mail the letters, put it out of her power to recall them, and then it would be done.

It was nearly dawn before she finished. But it was done. Her decision was made. She had come to greater clarity, and a kind of calm, while she wrote. The issues had become clearer as she outlined them to her parents. She did not tell them that she felt they were wrong to have asked this of her, only tried to explain why she could not do it.

For David, whose heart would not be affected, she merely said that she had made a mistake, that she would return his ring and gifts when she returned to New York. That she was sorry not to have known her own mind sooner. Then she took his ring off.

In bare feet, but still in the maroon dress, Caroline picked up the two letters and the key to her suite, and went downstairs to the reception desk. The night clerk was chatting to a man lounging in an armchair, whom she took to be hotel security. The latter sat up and looked at her with astonishment, but the clerk behind the desk conveyed the impression that nothing a foreign tourist did could surprise him.

"Good—" he eyed her dress and quickly made his choice, "—evening, Madame."

"Good evening. I just want to make sure that these letters go in the first mail pickup this morning. Do you have stamps?"

"Certainly, Madame. Air mail?"

The transaction took a few minutes. She paid for the stamps, licked them and put them on the letters. "What time will they be picked up?"

He spoke to the security guard in Arabic. Then, "At six o'clock, Madame," he said.

Too soon for her to change her mind. Caroline took a deep, nervous breath, then let it out and lifted her hand from the letters. "Be sure that they go, please."

He nodded, but did not answer. "Good night, Madame."

As she stepped back inside the elevator, the security guard got to his feet. Watching him through the gap in the closing doors, Caroline frowned absently. She had seen the guard before, but not at the hotel. Where?

When the elevator had gone, the man who had been lounging in the chair approached the reception desk and put his hand out. With some reluctance, the desk clerk handed him the two letters. "Is she in trouble?" he asked.

The other man did not answer. He was whistling absently through his teeth as he examined the two envelopes. After a moment he slipped them into his pocket. "If she asks you, the letters were picked up with the first post."

"She seems a very nice woman, what has she done?" the desk clerk asked unhappily.

"You are better off knowing nothing," said the other man.

She fell asleep immediately, her heart light for the first time since she had heard of David's proposal. In her dreams she bathed in a clear pool, using a beautiful bar of transparent blue soap, shaped like one of the tiles on Sultaness Halimah's mosque, that Kaifar gave her.

"She tried to telephone New York more than twenty times between midnight and four o'clock this morning," said the assistant secretary, laying the written report on the desk in front of Prince Karim.

Prince Karim made no response. Prince Rafi sat up, startled. "She did?"

"She was of course unable to get through." Jamil smiled. "And she sent these." He set down two letters, addressed in the English alphabet, stamped and marked Air Mail.

"We must open them!" Rafi said, reaching out a hand, but Prince Karim wordlessly stopped him. Silence fell in the room as he gazed down at the two envelopes under his hand.

"One to her fiancé, one to her mother," he observed.

"She has found something out," Prince Rafi warned. "What has she found out?"

Prince Karim shook his head. "She has found out nothing."

"Open the letters, and be sure."

His brother lifted one of the letters. His other hand hovered over the flap with uncharacteristic uncertainty.

"You can't afford scruples in this, Karim! If she has found out, who knows what she will do! She may run."

The prince shook his head and laid the letter down unopened. "She has found out nothing. There is no need to read them."

"Is she in love with your—this chauffeur of yours?"

Karim's eyebrows went up. "In love? No."

"And the chauffeur? Is he a little in love with her?"

"Of course not."

"You sound very certain."

The eyebrows came majestically down. "Of course I am certain. Do you imagine that I can be mistaken about such a thing?"

"Oh, easily. And if you were mistaken, you know—it would ruin everything."

"There is no love in the case."

"If there were," Prince Rafi pursued, "the result might be very unpredictable. If, for example, Kaifar were to put the girl's interests above Prince Karim's at a critical moment."

Prince Karim's eyes darkened with momentary doubt as he looked at his brother. "It would be disastrous," he agreed slowly. Then he recovered himself. "But it will not happen."

"It must be done today."

Prince Karim stared at nothing.

"Nasir has obtained an appointment for today, Karim. Do you hear?"

"What? Yes, I hear. It will be done today."

Eight

She slept for an hour or two, but a persistent bird woke her. Caroline got up and went down to the hotel restaurant for an early breakfast. She was tired from the lack of sleep, as well as emotionally drained and exhausted by the psychological journey she had made.

How long would it take for her letters to get there? She hoped they would reach home before she did.

The thought of seeing Kaifar, in her newly free state, made her unexpectedly nervous. But she had no number where she could reach him and he would turn up at the hotel at ten, as usual. At nine-thirty Caroline slipped a cotton dress over her swimsuit and a book into her voluminous beach bag. At reception, her heart pounding as if she were embarking on some spy adventure, she handed over a note for Kaifar telling him that she meant to take it easy and would spend the day alone. He could have the day off.

She put her ring into the safe box that each guest was

given, and stopped to purchase some suntan lotion and a few other things in the hotel shop. Then she set off down the white staircase that led down the outside of the hotel to the beach.

From this angle the white hotel was magnificent, a series of arches, tiled terraces and domed towers on several levels leading down to a golden sand beach and a smooth turquoise sea. The beach, backed by a palm forest, stretched for miles around the wide curving bay. On the beach in front of the hotel was an enclosure with a pool and a fountain, loungers, umbrellas, and leafy green plants, where a few hotel guests were already stretched out, but Caroline bypassed this and wandered down to the water's edge. To the left along the beach there were one or two smaller hotels; a couple of miles away she saw the towers of the city. To the right, in the distance, the bay curved to a point and then disappeared. No other building was visible, but the glint of sunlight on glass hinted at the presence of houses here and there hidden in the trees.

She turned in that direction, paddling barefoot through the water and the faintly hissing foam as the waves gently kissed the soft sand beneath her feet. The sun was already hot, the sky a deep blue miracle. There was no one on the beach ahead of her. Even in remote West Barakat this, she knew, was only because of the relatively early hour. She would enjoy her solitude while she had it.

She walked for half a mile and then unstrapped the small umbrella and the beach mat from the beach bag and staked out her little territory just beyond the reach of the highest waves. She could hear the gulls overhead, other birds in the trees behind her, the soft swish of the waves; nothing else.

She felt so free. Freer than at any moment since her brother died. What a fool she had been—rushing into the future blindly, refusing to look, because if she had looked, she would have had to turn away from it, and that would have displeased the parents she had never been able to please. She had snatched at her chance to make them love her, but she would not try anymore. She would be herself from now on.

Whatever Kaifar did now, she owed him enormous gratitude. Whatever they now became to each other, he had saved her, by forcing her to look at the truth. Exhausted and yet filled with the new energy of spiritual freedom, Caroline lay back under the shadow of the umbrella and breathed deeply of the sea air.

She was alone, and free. A couple some distance away were looking out to sea with binoculars, but they were not close enough to disturb her solitude. Smiling, Caroline closed her eyes and let the soft sound of the sea lullaby her to sleep.

When she awoke, suddenly opening her eyes without stirring, Kaifar was sitting on the sand beside her, in a dark boxer swimsuit, his knees drawn up, gazing out at the gulf. She lay looking at him without speaking, taking in the sight of his dark, muscular body, its beautiful proportions, the black hair curling lightly on his chest, arms and legs, springing thickly from his scalp. His profile showed strength in forehead, nose, chin and jaw—a man who would be firm in friendship as well as in enmity, a man used to making decisions, to taking responsibility. A man of truth and honesty.

She loved him. The information came to her as gently and naturally as the waves climbed up the sand, flowing up in her from some hidden recess, flooding her being in one sweet rush and then receding, leaving her breathless.

As if drawn by her feeling, he turned his head and looked down at her. They were immediately locked by each other's eyes. Without a word, Kaifar bent over her and kissed her on the mouth.

His mouth was tender, soft, barely brushing her lips that ever since last night had been waiting for this touch to be repeated, and the sweetness of the kiss exploded on her lips and through her body. Nothing had ever tasted so right to her heart, or so delicious to her senses, as Kaifar's kiss in that moment. He lifted his head a few inches and they smiled into each other's eyes for a long moment in which question and answer seemed the same.

"You look so different without your beard," Caroline murmured inconsequently, reaching up to run her fingers over his jaw. He was even more devastatingly attractive now. His chin was strong and firm, his lips sensuously beautiful, making her want to kiss them again.

He acknowledged her comment with a raised eyebrow and a smile. His eyes glinted at her as he rested on one elbow beside her. He pulled at a curl and bent to kiss it. Then he kissed her cheek, her eyes, her forehead, her temple. Caroline melted under the gentle assault of feeling that arose in her in the wake of his kisses, revelled in the warmth that radiated from his body, the smell of his heat, the nearness of his bare skin. Her body yearned towards him, her cells helplessly stirred into life by the powerful magnet that was his being.

She lifted her arms up around his neck, pressing her hungry hands against his sun-hot skin. In urgent response his arm went around her waist, drawing her up, and her breasts, covered by the thinnest layer of blue Lycra, brushed against his chest. She heard breath hiss between his teeth as Kaifar struggled for control, and then his mouth came down on hers, not lightly now, not gently, but with a ferocity that set a torch of sensation to her nerve endings.

His instant arousal was hard, huge and hurting against

the niche where body met thigh, and even as she grunted with the unexpected discomfort of its pressure against her soft flesh, her deep femininity gloried in it, for what it meant, and what it promised. His arm went under her shoulders, his hand cupped her head, and he kissed her with hungry desperation.

After a long moment, he lifted his lips and looked down at her. His hand gently drew a lock of hair out of her eyes. "I forget where we are," he muttered. He lifted himself away from her till he was on his side by her, propping himself up on one elbow, his look half smiling, half burning.

They didn't speak, merely smiled with the secret knowledge of lovers. Kaifar's left hand slipped under hers and he lifted it to his mouth. He kissed it once, twice, and then, in a change so sudden she blinked, his eyebrows snapped together, his grip tightened unbearably and he looked down at her hand.

"You have taken off your engagement ring."

As he gazed at her hand she could not see the expression in his eyes, but only the dark furrow of thick black eyebrows almost meeting. But she knew that he was not pleased.

All he wanted was a few nights of sex, she reminded herself. If he knew what choice she had made, might he withdraw out of fear of the consequences? How would he treat her if he knew how deep it had gone with her? Suddenly she could not bear for him to know what it meant to her, how far she had lost herself with him.

Her heart tearing at her like a dull knife, she bent forward and dusted the sand from her calves. "I left it at the hotel because I was coming to the beach, Kaifar," she lied. "Try to rid yourself of the conviction that I'm so smitten with your dark eyes that I'd throw over the Marriage of the Year for you!"

He raised his head and looked into her eyes. "It was not my eyes, but your honour that I thought of," he said, with a gentle contempt that made her want to slap his face.

"I'm going in the water," she said, and stood up and ran the few yards into the gentle blue waves.

The sea was as warm as the body of a loving mother. She entered it without any physical shock, as naturally as going home. She flung herself forward and dived under, surfaced to swim with furious speed for a few minutes, then rolled over and floated on her back. The water buoyed her up and she lay in its embrace effortlessly, blinking up at the sky through the mix of tears and seawater clustering in her lashes.

Kaifar didn't love her. What should she do, feeling as she did? Snatch at the less than half loaf—the crumbs!— that were offered her? Take him on any terms? Or deny what both of them wanted out of fear of being more hurt by their parting afterwards?

She would suffer at parting anyway, that much was already clear. Whatever happened over the next week, she would not board the plane home with a whole heart. Would the pain be more, or less, if she let him love her under the conditions he had just tacitly set? He had promised her physical pleasure, and she was sure he was expert enough with women to make good on the promise. The mere thought of his intimate touch melted her.

Smoothly as a seal, the subject of her thoughts surfaced beside her. He smiled at her, the water sparkling on his lashes and in his hair, and his arms went around her waist, pulling her upright against him. Air rushed into her lungs in a response that she could not disguise. Her heart was thumping.

He was determined not to allow her room to think, but thinking was stupid, anyway, where the battle had already been lost. She had been playing games with herself. She could not decide not to make love with Kaifar. He stirred her too deeply. He had only to touch her and blood, bone and being leapt in crazy response.

"Will you come with me now, Caroline?" he whispered. There could be no answer but yes.

Back on the beach, Kaifar pulled his strong, muscular legs into a pair of pale cotton trousers while Caroline absent-mindedly watched, a smile curving her lips. When he buttoned them, her gaze drew his, and he pulled her close with one arm around her waist and kissed her on the mouth. "Stop that," he said.

With a laugh she bent to her own dress and pulled it on over her head. When she emerged from the neckline, Kaifar had tossed his shirt around his neck and was putting down the beach umbrella.

A moment later they were striding along the beach towards the hotel. He led her past the pool and up the stairs, but in the courtyard forestalled her instinctive move towards the door, drawing her instead to the outer courtyard, where the Rolls was parked.

She resisted. "I want to go and change!" she said with a laugh. "I'm all covered with salt!"

His eyes were suddenly filled with an intense sexual impatience, as if he had been holding it in check and could no longer do so. "Then you will taste even more delicious!" he told her, bent to kiss her with passionate intensity, and, wrapping an arm around her, almost dragged her to the car.

Nine

Caroline knew as soon as he opened the door into the garden that Kaifar had brought her back to the place they had visited last night. But she asked no questions as he led her across the beautiful, shady garden, past a fountain and through a doorway leading upstairs. Then across the room where they had eaten last night, and to the cool, shaded bedroom.

She turned at once and went into his arms with a hunger she could hardly believe. "Kaifar," she murmured, kissing his parted lips, her arms wrapped around his neck, pressing her breasts against his naked chest, offering herself freely and openly. Her heart was aching for sheer joy, her body already thrumming with pleasure. She felt his arms around her and knew that no other arms could ever be so perfect for her. His body stirred passionately, and then he drew out of her arms, holding her slightly away.

"I have to leave you for a while," Kaifar murmured. "Please wait here."

It took her a moment to hear what she was hearing. "What?" she said, with an incredulous smile.

"Please. Caroline. There is something I must see to."

His body was hard. "Oh, yes!" she smiled. "There is!"

She took his hand in both of hers and smilingly drew him towards the bed.

His eyes were black with tormented passion. The look in them melted her over and over again. "I bought condoms in the hotel this morning," she whispered. "They're in my beach bag."

"Caroline."

She smiled at him with all the desire and passion of heart and spirit and body. "Kaifar, I promise to regret nothing. I promise not to blame you, I promise not to beg for what you can't give me. But this I know you can give me, and you want to." Suddenly confusion smote her. "Don't you? Don't you want me after all?"

With an oath he stepped towards her, and, his passion bursting all bounds, picked her up bodily and kissed her with a need that flamed through her. In the next moment she felt the silken coverlet under her and Kaifar's arms around her, his mouth possessively taking from hers all that she offered, and more.

He pressed her head between his hands, kissing her wildly, both of them drowning in sensation. She felt the muscles of the whole length of his body respond to her femininity—his arms overpowering and yet cradling her, his chest both firm and yielding against her breasts, his back strong yet trembling under her hands, his thighs stroking her with hungry heat—only the hard thrust of his sex against hers did not give against her softness, only that showed no promise that the lion would be gentle with the lamb.

Yet even that passionate hunger he could hold in check, and he stroked and caressed her as if determined to overwhelm her with more sensation than her system could bear.

She felt his hand at the hem of her cotton dress, pulling it up over her thighs, and he drew his mouth from hers and then lifted her body to urge the still-damp fabric up over her hips and breasts and then over her head. Underneath she wore her bikini, thin and clinging, that ruthlessly outlined her aroused nipples, and exposed most of her skin to his expert touch.

Kaifar held her, gently urging her body back against the bed again, then bent over her and kissed her shoulder, her tender neck, her throat. His hand drew the thin strap of her bathing suit down over her rounded shoulder, kissing the path it made so that she felt like a wanton. His tongue ran hungrily around the upper edge of the boned bra, seeking entry to the roundness that the fabric hid, until her whole body lay helplessly yearning for the touch of his tongue on her nipples.

With a suddenness that startled her, her breasts were freed from the confinement that kept her from his mouth; so sweet and entrancing was the touch of his mouth that she had not noticed his fingers at her back until the snap was open and he was drawing the bra gently away.

Her naked breasts shivered with the touch of the air, and with the expectation of his mouth, his tongue, his strong dark hand. His hand touched her first, cupping the sexual, sensual weight of her breast with passionate satisfaction, looking down at the beaded nipple for only a second before bending to take it between his lips.

Sensation shot through her with the touch of his hot, moist mouth, was heightened with every rasping stroke of his hungry tongue. She arched her back and whimpered with hungry yearning and felt by the rough tightening of his hand on her arm how nearly that sound brought him to the edge of his control. He lifted his mouth and pressed it wildly against her mouth again, as if to prevent her hungry, grateful cries.

His hand left her breast and moved with firm ownership down between her thighs. His eyes burned into hers as he took this intimate possession of her body, watching for her response, his jaw clenching as she moaned in the passionate surprise of her own body's unexpected rush of pleasure. In this moment, she *wanted* his ownership, she wanted him to stake his claim to exclusive rights, and she smiled at him because she knew that, in this moment, he wanted to own her, too.

He did not say it, but the firm possessive clasp of his hand told her. When he released that hold, it was only to take up another, only to let the firm soft pad of his thumb explore till he found the place where his touch made her eyes close, and her throat open on a soundless gasp.

Her thighs parted involuntarily, and then his fingers shifted gently till they found the edge of her bikini, and then the heat of his hand was inside against her skin, against the softest flesh of her body, sliding down against the sensitive heart of her physical being so that she gasped and her legs melted apart, offering herself to his conquering exploration.

His fingers stroked her, and everywhere he touched, she turned to melting liquid, to honey, easing his passage. Lazily, he drew the hot honey over all the secret enfoldings of her female self, over the pearl hidden within. She leapt against the silky sheets as sensation burned out from under his hand to all her nerves, exciting every inch of skin, every cell, every pore, every part of her.

The sensation rolled over and through her in waves of mounting pleasure and then burst in a little fireball that sent heat all through her, all around her. She clung to him, opening her mouth under his; and he sucked the inner softness of her lips as if the honey he had released in her could be tasted there, and his hand rocked with her rocking response to release.

When he felt the pleasure subside in her, his hand drew the bikini bottoms erotically aside, exposing the flesh that had been hidden, and she opened her eyes to see his hungry gaze fix on her for one second before his head bent and his mouth moved to nestle beside his clenched hand, kissing the folds of tender flesh that now were all that hid the pearl of pleasure.

With a gasp of hungry surprise she told him that she knew what he meant to do, and how desperate she was for him to do it. Then the heat of his tongue, gently teasing her soft flesh, drew blackness down over her vision, and now there was only the spangle of stars that danced to this magic touch.

How long the dance went on she never afterwards knew. She only knew that each release came more quickly, and each release, conversely, built up a different tension in her, making her an addict of pleasure, needing more and more the more she was given.

She knew that he paused to draw off her bikini bottoms at last, knew that he threw off his own clothes, knew that the skin of his arms and chest was naked against hers as he pressed her legs even further apart, lifting her body as his mouth descended hungrily again, knew that the pleasure that had built in her was too much to bear. She whimpered, moaned, cried both with and for release. Never had she wanted so much, she had never known need like this. Never before had any man brought her to this point where to turn back would have been impossible.

She was begging him, with her body, with her voice. With moans and whimpers she told him of her need, until at last he was driven beyond the reach of his own control. She felt him tremble as he fitted the condom to his engorged, hungry body, and, her eyes fluttering open, she groaned with a mixture of fear and deep animal response as she saw what was to be her fate. Then he was close above her, his chest powerful over hers, his thighs pushing against hers, his sex demanding entry.

Then for one instant fear overcame desire. "Kaifar!" she pleaded. "Oh, please—!"

"Yes," he growled. "I know, Caroline. Trust me."

But he did not know. Not until, with those words, he pushed his way in past the barrier he had not expected to find, not until he heard her cry of joyful completion mingling with the high whimper of pain, not until he saw the wide surprise of her passion-drugged eyes, did he know what she had given him.

Even in the extreme of passionate need for her that he had reached, the understanding stopped him. His hand slipped under her neck, and he ruthlessly cupped her tossing head and held her firm to face his searching gaze.

"Caroline!"

She smiled, seeing him there in the mists above her. "Kaifar," she breathed. "Oh, oh, *oh!* Isn't it wonderful? Oh, but it hurts! Oh, push in again, oh, it's heaven, oh, I've never felt anything so wonderful in my life."

"Caroline!" he said again. "*Allah,* do you give me this?"

But he had to thrust into her again, and she was lost, rolling on waves of pleasure and sensation that robbed her of speech and hearing, and everything except the power to experience that intermingling of soul and body that we call Union.

"I understand you have something to show me," David Percy said flatly.

The swarthy-skinned man stood with a large velvet box held close to his chest. It wasn't unusual for these people to imagine that some family heirloom or stolen artefact was the equivalent of the Inca treasure, and David was almost sure he was wasting his time. But the man had insisted on a personal meeting; refused to show any underling the piece in question. Now he seemed in no hurry, though, simply standing there staring at him from intent dark eyes.

David Percy raised his hands and dropped them down on his desk. "All right, let's see what you've got. Take a seat."

The man obediently moved forward to the chair in front of the desk and sank into it. Then he lifted the velvet box and slid it slowly over the table. David Percy reached for it with poorly disguised impatience. He hated the foreign courtesies these people always wanted to impose in situations like this; he always figured it was manipulative. Anyway, people who came to him like this were either thieves or dirt poor, having lost what they were born with, so it was a bit much for him to expect to be treated like some kind of potentate.

"Let's have a look," he said, opening the box with practised ease. Then he froze with surprise.

"What the hell is this?"

Of its own accord his hand went to the green jewel and picked it up. He stared fixedly at it for a moment, and then relaxed. He raised his eyebrows at the seller. "Well?"

"Perhaps you have heard of the Jewel Seal of Shakur," said the man softly.

"I've heard of it," David Percy replied flatly.

"My employer is offering—"

"Not interested!"

Nasir raised his eyebrows enquiringly as David Percy tossed down the stone and flung himself back in his chair.

"That's a fake!"

Nasir smiled and inclined his head. "But of course it is a fake, Mr. Percy. And naturally you, of all people, would know it," he said with a subtlety that didn't impress David one bit.

"I don't know what the hell you think you mean!" he returned, his jaw very stiff. "Why should I know it more than anyone else?"

"But you are a great expert, Mr. Percy. What else could I mean?"

"I don't buy copies."

"Nevertheless, my employer hopes that you would like to purchase this one. An exchange would satisfy him."

David crossed one knee over the other. "Get out, and take your fake emerald with you."

Nasir sat without moving. The look in his eyes was one of contempt, but David Percy chose not to recognize it. "Although he hoped to find you in a more—honourable— frame of mind, the possibility did occur to my employer that you would not be eager to make such an exchange without encouragement. There is in my employer's possession another treasure, Mr. Percy. Perhaps you would be interested in that."

He reached into his breast pocket and extracted a photograph, placed it face down on the desk, and slid it towards the dealer. David watched with a half smile, half frown of reluctant interest. Any sweetener from this particular source was likely to be an extremely tempting piece. He plucked up the photograph and turned it over.

He stiffened.

"What the hell is this?"

In his hand was a photograph of Caroline Langley.

"You have been quoted as saying, I believe, that this jewel was the prize of your private collection, as the Emerald Seal was of my employer's. It has now come into my employer's hands. He feels certain that you will wish to have such a rare and perfect jewel restored to you." He paused, but there was no reaction. "Although he admires this jewel very much—" Nasir gently indicated the photograph "—he has asked me to tell you that if you will pass into my hands his jewel, at present in your possession, he will undertake to return your own treasure in due course. If you reveal the details of this offer to the press or police, my employer warns you that your own jewel, Mr. Percy, will disappear from the earth."

In the early evening she woke up singing. She could smell delicious food, and she stretched languorously while a smile pulled irresistibly at the corners of her mouth. Oh, what a lover she had found! She thought of her various friends warning her that she was missing vital years of her sexuality—she had missed nothing, because Kaifar had given her everything in a single day. She did not need to compare him with anyone else to know that the magic that had happened for them was rare, beautiful, unmissable. Even if one week with him had to last her the rest of her life, she could not have turned away.

Afterwards, lying there, holding her, he asked, "Caroline, why did you not tell me?"

"Would it have changed anything?"

He didn't answer. "How are you a virgin?"

"Why not?"

"But you are...twenty-two, twenty-three?"

"I'm twenty-three in a couple of weeks," she agreed.

He stroked her forehead, watched a lock of her hair cleave spontaneously to his finger. "Why have you had no lover, Caroline?"

She shrugged. "Just basic self-preservation, Kaifar. I made up my mind when I was sixteen that I wasn't going to engage in casual sex."

"And why have you changed this now?"

That was unanswerable unless she told him the truth. She had changed nothing. It was not casual sex for her. She had fallen in love and had made love with him because she loved him. That was the bargain she had made with herself at sixteen—no sex until she was deeply and honestly in love with a man whom she wanted to spend her life with.

She smiled at him. "When you really want to know the answer to that question, I might tell you."

His dark eyes clouded with trouble. He said no more, only drew her into his arms. After a few minutes she had fallen deeply asleep.

She heard china and cutlery clinking in the other room, and got up. Discovering that she was naked, she blushed, smiled, and reached for her bikini and sundress, now lying neatly across a beautiful antique chair.

Earlier, she had not taken in the magnificence of the bedroom, but now she looked around her and was amazed. It was like something out of an illustrated copy of *The Arabian Nights,* with white stucco walls, leaded windows looking out over the garden, intricately carved wooden panels decorating numerous arches and niches; spacious, airy, full of statues, paintings, and silk carpets. The hangings on the bed were gold tapestry.

Where on earth was she? She had imagined that it was Kaifar's apartment or house, but could he possibly own such magnificence? Perhaps he had inherited it from his courtier father?

She stepped through a door into the bathroom, if it could be called that. She had never seen so much beautiful marble, or such a large room devoted entirely to cleansing the human body. The bathtub was a square pool in the marble floor with steps leading down the sides, big enough for twenty people. There were beautiful gold-plated antique showers along one wall, there were mirrors and a stack of thick white towels...

When she came out, the food smells were stronger than before, and she opened the door to the passage and followed it along to the room where they had eaten the first night Kaifar had brought her here. Through an archway she saw a long expanse of black and white marble tiles, and silk-covered sofas and chairs, and more carpets. His father, she told herself, must have been a very important man.

A man in a white shirt and trousers was putting the finishing touches to a small Western-style table with chairs by a window overlooking the garden, where sunset was turning everything gold. He sensed her barefoot approach and turned. *"Salaam, Madame,"* he said with a formal bow. He said more, but nothing she could follow.

"Salaam," she said.

"Please," he enunciated, and indicated by sign language that she should sit on the cushions surrounding the low table she and Kaifar had sat at—a long, long time ago. Now she saw that there was a tray of drinks and wine, and several bowls of exotic tidbits set there. She sank down and took something from a bowl as he offered it.

"Where is Kaifar?" she asked, crunching the delicately spiced and herbed morsel. Delicious.

The man's eyes widened. "Kaifar?"

"The—" How should she describe him? *The man who*

brought me here? The owner of the place? Did he own the place? Was this magnificent apartment Kaifar's own apartment?

"Madame laike wahin?" Another charming, liquid smile.

It took her a moment to realize he had spoken English. "Yes, thank you."

He lifted the white inquiringly and she nodded. He poured the liquid into a gold-brushed goblet of heavy crystal that would not have been disdained by a sultan. Caroline relaxed for a few minutes, then, when Kaifar did not appear, felt that the obvious course would be to go and change into something more suitable at the hotel.

She set down her wine and stood up. "I would like to go to the hotel now," she informed the waiter. He stared at her with blank incomprehension. "Hotel!" she said, pointing to herself. "Go. Now." She mimed a steering wheel.

His eyes wide, the man shook his head. "No go, Madame." He raised his hands parallel with the floor and waggled them to indicate that she should remain here. "Eat." He mimed eating, waved his hands at the table he was laying so beautifully.

Caroline nodded. "I'll come back to eat," she said, more for her sake than for his, since he clearly didn't understand a word. Anyway, he was unlikely to be able to take her to the hotel. She would walk till she found a cab.

She got up and went into the bedroom for her beach bag. When she came out again, the man was standing waiting for her, looking worried and disappointed. "I'll come back in half an hour," she said, pointing to her wrist and miming thirty, then strode to the door that led to the staircase down to the garden.

Behind her the waiter called out, but they were unlikely

to understand each other, and the faster she went, the sooner she would be back.

There was a man sitting in the garden. He sat up with a start as Caroline came out of the door, and got to his feet. With a nod, Caroline walked to the arched door in the high garden wall and pulled the handle. It was locked.

"Madame, Madame!"

She turned to face the waiter and the other man, both moving agitatedly in her direction, calling out remonstrations in Arabic that she could not understand. She smiled calmly but with firmness of purpose.

"Open this door, please!"

"Not go, not go, Madame!" protested the waiter. He pushed his hands at the door to indicate that it was closed and must remain so. He spoke to her in rapid, incomprehensible Arabic, and in exasperation she waved her own hands to block the stream.

"I don't understand a word you're saying," she told him. She waved a hand to the door. "Unlock the door," she said, miming the action.

The other man turned to him and said something, and the waiter nodded violently. "Prince!" he said, happy to have the word. "Prince come!"

Caroline stared at him. "Prince? Who is Prince?"

"You...you...wahin!" He pointed upstairs to the lattice window where she had sat to drink wine and, without touching her, tried to shepherd her back to the doorway that led there.

Suddenly, Caroline was afraid. Where was Kaifar, what was this place, who were these men, and above all, why were they trying to keep her here? In spite of the evening warmth, she began to shiver. Ignoring their gently waving arms, she turned and pulled at the handle to the door in the wall again. The door was very firmly locked. Trying to remain cool, she turned back to face the men. "Open this door!" she commanded.

Again they babbled excuses and explanations. Then, for a strange moment, aware of her utter incomprehension, they abruptly fell silent. Into the silence, from outside the walls, fell the sound of footsteps. With a suddenness that electrified her two captors, Caroline flung herself at the thick wooden door and began to kick and bang on it.

"Help! Help! Let me out! Help, please help!" she screamed. "Police! Police!"

Her anxious captors started their babble again, making soothing and reassuring noises which did neither. Caroline screamed again, and then there was a knock on the door and a voice called out urgently in Arabic.

Her captors shouted a reply, and then, to her sighing relief, the man who had been sitting in the garden reached into his pocket and pulled out a massive iron key, ludicrously on the same chain as a tiny brass one. Caroline stepped to one side as he approached the door, holding her breath as he used first the black key and then the golden one.

The door opened inwards. A man stepped through the opening, and she had just begun to babble her thanks when she noticed two things that closed her throat, choking off her words. The first was that the man who entered was talking to the men in a familiar way. The second was that he had in his hands her luggage from the hotel.

Ten

Her heart stopped beating. The man slipped through the door and blocked the opening with his body as the others pushed it firmly closed and locked it again.

Caroline stood trying to calm her panic, trying not to lose her reason as all three men now turned to face her. "Who are you?" she demanded in a hoarse voice. "What are you doing with my things?"

She did not expect an answer, but the third man, after passing her luggage to the waiter and muttering some command that sent him upstairs with it, said, "I am sorry, Madame. Please do not be afraid. No one will hurt you here."

"I would like to go, then, please."

He shrugged expressively. "Madame, you must wait here."

"What *must* I wait for, and where exactly is 'here'?" Caroline demanded, trying to sound angry rather than terrified. Her heart seemed to be choking her.

He had a rapid exchange in Arabic with the man with the keys.

"The prince is late. He intended to be here. He is coming soon. He will talk to you. He will explain."

"The prince?" She had thought it was a name. "What prince? What are you talking about?"

"His Serene Highness Prince Karim, Emir of West Barakat, Madame. I am Jamil, his assistant private secretary."

"Where is the man who brought me here? Where is Kaifar?"

His eyes went blank, and suddenly she was terrified. "What have you done to Kaifar?" she cried. She could hear how desperate her voice sounded, and thought, *I shouldn't show them my feelings, they will use them against us,* and fought down the need to know Kaifar's fate.

"I can tell you nothing, Madame. His Serene Highness will explain all when he comes. He asks that you wait. Please, you will like to dress. The chef makes dinner for you. Very, very good food. Prince Karim's number first chef."

She could almost laugh at the ludicrous mention of food in such a moment. But in one thing the man was right. Whoever and whatever was coming, and she certainly did not believe that it was a prince, she didn't want to face it in a sea- and salt-stained cotton sundress and a bikini. Caroline turned and allowed herself to be led back upstairs and into the bedroom, where her bags had already been placed. She locked the door from the inside and breathed for what felt like the first time in minutes.

In curious incongruity with her surroundings, she dressed in jeans, a T-shirt, and sneakers. Her neatly packed things, she noted, included the box with her engagement ring. Whoever had picked up her bags must have been given the contents of her safety deposit box, but her passport and money were missing. She closed her eyes against the sick terror that arose in her—no one would miss her, no one would ask where she was! When would David or her mother try to phone? Between her mother and herself was an agreement that Caroline would do the phoning. With David there had been no discussion at all, and once he got her letter… It might be days before anyone set up an alarm.

"I'll go down and wait for his Serene Highness outside," she informed Jamil when she emerged, hiding the wolfish fear that was gnawing at her. He made no attempt to stop her, but as soon as she came down she saw that the guard was still on duty in the garden. There would be no quick escape up a tree and over the wall with him there.

She wandered up and down in the magnificent garden, oblivious to the sight and the perfume of the thousands of blossoms, the music of waterfalls and birdsong, her stomach and heart clenching with that deep, primitive, gnawing fear that made her almost physically sick. What would happen to her? What would they do to her? What did they want? Why were they telling her the ridiculous lies about the prince? Was it the beginnings of psychological torture, would they go on to try to undermine her mental stability?

She was a hostage. That was all she knew. Money, they must want money from David. The thought terrified her. What would they do if they did not get it? But surely David would—

One of the things that my wife will have to understand is that I am completely opposed in principle to paying kidnappers ransom.

Oh, God, what would they do to her if he refused? Oh, please, please let David change his mind! Please let him pay what they asked! *David,* she pleaded silently in the gloom, *you have so much money, and I have only one life.*

She thought bitterly that the timing of her letter could

not have been worse. Would anyone believe that she was
not engaged to David now?

Twilight turned into night, and the stars were filling the
sky before she heard the sound of a car engine in the lane
outside. The car stopped, the engine died, and then there
were footsteps.

Her heart beating in her head and ears with a force that
deafened her, Caroline moved to the door in the guard's
wake and stood waiting as he unlocked it. In the shadowy
light it took a moment for her fear-filled heart to recognize
the man who entered. Then a cry of relief tore from her
throat.

"Kaifar!" He turned a gravely smiling face towards her
as she ran pell-mell into his arms. "Kaifar, I thought—I
thought they'd killed you or something! Quick, before he
closes the door again! Something weird is going on! We've
got to get out of here!"

"Caroline," he said softly, and then she noticed the curious fact that the guard who had opened the door was
bowing. "I am sorry, I was delayed."

Behind her, Jamil had arrived. "Good evening, Your
Highness," he said, and she felt rather than saw the quick
negative shake of Kaifar's head.

Stepping back out of his hold, Caroline began to laugh,
half with confused fright, half with relief.

"Kaifar, what on earth is going on?" she demanded in
a nervous babble. "Don't play games with me! Who are
these men? They got my luggage from the hotel, and they
wouldn't let me leave! They—"

He stilled her by the simple expedient of putting his hand
on her arm. "I am sorry that you have been frightened,
Caroline. There is much to explain to you. There is a meal
prepared for us. Come upstairs and I will explain."

She stood firm under the gentle urging of his hand while

the ice of a different kind of fear coursed through her veins. She gazed up into dark eyes visible only by the reflected glitter of a distant light.

"No," she said, trying to keep panic out of her voice. "No, I want to leave this place now. Let's go somewhere else for dinner."

He looked at her, and the night was cold and empty around her, and all of nature seemed to die. "Caroline, do not ask this, but come upstairs with me."

"Open the door, Kaifar," she said. What kind of fool had she been, and why had she trusted him, knowing nothing about him? Oh, God, and what was he going to do to her?

"I cannot do that," he informed her sadly.

She stared at him while a million unnamed dreams shattered into dust. "Am I a hostage, Kaifar?"

He looked steadily at her. She closed her eyes. Strange how her eyes could be so burning when all of her was frozen.

"You bastard," she said without emotion.

"It is natural that you will feel anger."

She ignored that. "Your hostage, or someone else's?"

"Mine," he said, with that possessive note in his voice that only hours ago she had found erotic. Not now.

"Why do they say you are a prince? Are you a prince?" Her voice seemed to be coming from a distance. She had no feelings, except that she was cold as death now. Her blood seemed to have stopped moving.

"Caroline, come upstairs where we can talk in comfort," he urged again. "There is much to tell you, much for you to understand."

"Do I have any choice in the matter?"

He stood silent for a long moment, while she heard the sound of his deep breathing. All around them she suddenly

heard and smelled the garden and the night again. For the
past few minutes she had been in a sensory void, but now
the world came back. Its presence hurt her. The precious,
beautiful world with all its colours and scents and love and
joy—how long would she know it?

"Caroline," he said at last.

"If I have a choice, Kaifar, my choice is to leave this
place now. If I have no choice, I await Your Majesty's
order. But I will not pretend that I go anywhere willingly
in your company."

"Then I order you upstairs," he replied calmly, and in
that moment she almost believed that he was a prince of
the realm, so easily did command sit on him.

Her heart suddenly returned, too, a bitter and burning
organ within her that spread misery throughout her system.
Without a word she turned and preceded him through the
little arched entry that only a few hours ago had seemed
like the doorway to magic to her.

The food was brought to the table as soon as they appeared. It smelled delicious, and reluctantly Caroline could
feel hunger stirring in her after the depletion of her nervous
energy over the past hour. But although she sat when the
waiter pulled out her chair, she shook her head when Kaifar
offered her the basket of bread.

"I would like to hear your explanation, please," she said
coldly, her hands folded resolutely in her lap.

"Eat, Caroline," he urged. "You have eaten nothing
since morning, I think."

"I will not eat in your company."

He looked at her assessingly from under his brows, then
lifted his head. He guessed immediately what she meant to
do. "You will eat first, or you will get no explanation."

"I'm not hungry."

He leaned a little towards her. "You are hungry. If you mean to go on a hunger strike, Caroline, you will do it without knowing the reasons for what I do, or anything of your situation."

For a moment she sat staring at him. But she knew without even thinking that, while she might overcome the need for food, she could not withstand the need to know. That torment would be unbearable. She *had* to hear what was happening, what her fate would be.

She swore helplessly at him and took a piece of *naan*. He helped her to fill her plate with all the delicious things on offer, and filled his own. Then, as they began to eat, he smiled. But nothing in her rose to meet that smile. She felt bruised. She gazed stonily at him.

"All right, I'm eating." *The condemned man ate a hearty meal.* "So why don't you tell me what you have in mind for me? Is this meal my last? If so, I feel I should make a particular effort to enjoy it, in spite of the company I find myself in."

"It is not your last meal. You will not be hurt or harmed by anyone," he said, ignoring the bright sarcasm and speaking to the terror that lurked underneath her tone. In spite of herself she believed him. She reminded herself coldly to believe no reassurances, nothing that he said. To promise and then break a promise was a form of psychological torture.

"Caroline, do you remember the story of the three sons of the Sheikh of Barakat?"

"How will I ever forget."

"I am one of those three sons. My name is Karim. Sheikh Daud was my father. When he died, this part of Barakat, now called West Barakat, fell to my lot. In addition, into my care was given one of the royal treasures, the emerald seal of our ancestor Shakur. This seal has an important superstition surrounding it. It is believed that the monarch will reign only as long as Shakur's Jewel is in his possession.''

"Fascinating," she informed him.

He ignored the sarcasm. ''The tribes share this traditional belief. If the seal were lost or stolen, many would fear the future, but some would see in this their opportunity to challenge my kingship and that of my brothers. Civil war would be the almost inevitable result. Many lives would be lost. Many would suffer. Surrounding nations might see in this weakness opportunity for them also.''

"Thank you for this little insight into the problems of Sheikhdom," she began. ''I suppose—''

He overrode her as if she had not spoken. ''Your fiancé, David Percy, stole the Great Jewel Seal of Shakur from my treasury and replaced it with a counterfeit.''

Knocked out of her mocking pose, Caroline gasped and stared. ''What?'' she breathed.

"He bribed—blackmailed—one of the Keepers of the Treasury in a way that I will not describe to you, and in this way first an impression of the seal was made and copied by a jeweller, and then the copy was substituted and the true seal smuggled out.''

"I don't believe you!''

"It was very carefully done. It took my people much time, and a painstaking investigation, to trace this crime to David Percy's door, and then to learn that to take back the jewel by stealth would be impossible without danger to life.''

She was shaking. "I refuse to believe this." She had known they would try to undermine her world, make her lose faith, and this would certainly shake her if she believed it. As far as she knew, not even his business rivals had ever challenged David's professional integrity.

"It is natural that a woman should believe in the integrity of the man she has promised to marry, as natural as that he should believe in her honour," Prince Karim said gently.

She felt the tip of the whip under his words. "Oh, I see!" she said with bitter mockery. "I screwed you for a bit of fun on the side, so I have no right to disbelieve you when you accuse David of theft! And you, Kaifar—or should I say Your Royal Highness?—where are your morals in all this?"

"I did not expect to find you a virgin."

She stared at him, then looked away, shaking her head with disbelief. "Why didn't you just kidnap me, why did you have to play games with my emotions? Was it all part of your revenge?"

"No. I am sorry, Caroline. It was my hope to bring you here without violence and keep you here in ignorance. I did not expect to have to explain to you. I hoped in this way to avoid the terrors that a kidnapping would cause you. But I was detained and my staff did not fully understand."

"Oh, you're all heart!"

"It was not my intention to—"

"Your intention!" she sneered. "It was your intention to do whatever it took! I suppose you have some psychological advisor who told you that if you could make me fall for you by pretending to be attracted and then show me what your motives were I'd be instantly destabilized! There's no faith in you, so there's no faith in anyone, is that what I'm supposed to feel now?"

He waited, watching her steadily through this outburst. When she stopped and stared back at him, her jaw set, he asked, "Caroline, what do you imagine then, the truth to be? Why do you think I hold you hostage?"

"I have no idea. Maybe you sold your prize whatsit to David for a massive price and now the word has gotten out among the people and you're trying to force him to restore it to you for free! How do I even know you're who you say you are? Why should I believe you're Prince Karim? It could just be your way of undermining me. Maybe tomorrow you'll tell me you're a famous Barakati gangster with a reputation for slowly dismembering the women he takes hostage."

She could feel tears burning their way up in her and clenched her jaw to prevent their finding a way out.

"It is not my intention to undermine you. I will give you proof that I am Prince Karim if that is what you need."

At that moment the waiter came into the room, and Kaifar spoke to him in Arabic. The man nodded, set down the tray, and pulled a small coin purse out of his pocket. He extracted a piece of paper money—20 dirhams, Caroline noted distantly—carefully unfolded it, and placed it on the table with a small bow.

"Look at the portrait, Caroline," Kaifar commanded.

She was already familiar with the colourful picture of the three princes. "I've seen it before."

"Look more closely," he urged.

It was true that one of the faces closely resembled Kaifar's. "That's supposed to be you, is it?" she said rudely. "You're not just some quick-buck artist who's noticed his uncanny resemblance to the prince and is making the most of it?"

He smiled and frowned simultaneously. "Caroline, you are in my palace."

She glanced around. That seemed to explain a lot. "Am I?"

"This is a private section of the ancient harem, used for centuries by visiting female heads of state. In the days of my grandfather Queen Victoria stayed in these rooms."

She seemed to lose all her strength suddenly. She

dropped her head and sat shaking it gently from side to side. "I don't care who you are."

"But of course you do. It is important that you should have the stability of knowing that what I tell you is true. Come."

He was on his feet as he spoke, giving some command to the waiter as he pulled Caroline's chair out for her, and she was up before she could refuse. As he led her along a corridor and unlocked a massive door at the end, she shrugged against the thrill of fear she felt. She was powerless now, and whatever he was going to do to her, it hardly mattered where.

She followed him through room after room, along endless corridors, all so beautifully decorated and ornately furnished that this had to be either a palace or a museum. Or both. She saw paintings on the walls that she recognized from postcards and reproductions, that took her breath away. She saw painted portraits of handsome bearded men in turbans and women in embroidered draperies with jewels the size of goose eggs adorning fingers and necks and ears and foreheads and noses. She saw pieces of furniture of the most astonishing workmanship and age.

And at last they were in front of a steel door with a modern electronic code-entry panel beside it, and Prince Karim was putting in a number. The door clunked open, and he pulled it wide for her, and Caroline stood on the threshold staring while her jaw went slack with wonder and amazement.

She had never seen so much jewellery in one place in her life. She had never known rubies and emeralds and sapphires and diamonds of such size existed outside of fairy tales. She recognized some as the originals of the portraits she had passed: an egg-sized cabochon emerald surrounded by a circlet of alternating rubies and diamonds, each one of which was almost the size of her own diamond solitaire; a sapphire as blue and entrancing as the night sky, and equally full of stars; pearls that glowed in matched perfection...

In the centre of one wall was a glass case, its bed of white satin empty. Prince Karim led her there. "This is where the Jewel Seal of Shakur has rested for many generations, since this palace was built."

"Where is the copy?" she asked, capitulating. She believed him now—not that David had been the author of the theft, but of everything pertaining to who Kaifar was, she was convinced. No other explanation was possible. However unbelievable, however dreamlike, she had to accept that her tour guide, Kaifar, was in fact the ruler of West Barakat.

"It is in New York. We wished first to give your—to give Mr. Percy the opportunity to make restitution without any reference to you, or any threat. We merely offered him the information that we knew of his involvement in the theft and a direct trade of his copy for my property. He refused."

"Well, of course he did! Your spies will have to accept that they made a mistake. It wasn't David." Yet some secret part of her thought about his coldness, and wondered if the thing she feared in David was a lack of conscience.

He looked at her, his eyes level, his jaw firm. "There has been no mistake, Caroline. I am sorry to be the one to tell you such things about your fiancé. Even without the proof we have, his name would have figured high on a list of suspects. David Percy is well known as a man who asks no embarrassing questions about title papers or export documents when he trades in the world's ancient treasures. His wealth is feared by every official of every country which has a heritage to protect for its citizens."

She made no reply, but stood with her head bent, gazing at nothing. She was beginning to believe it, and was that the way it worked? Your captors repeated and repeated a lie until it seemed to resonate with something in you that already knew? Was it true? She thought of some of the treasures David had showed her, her astonishment that such pieces could be found anywhere outside of a museum. She knew so little about David's world, and everything she knew he had taught her.

As if misunderstanding her silence, Karim moved to open the case beside her and took out a beautiful circlet that she had seen on one of the dark-eyed women in the portraits they had passed. Made of emeralds and diamonds, it had one central jewel and several smaller sprays to each side. Karim lifted it and placed it on her forehead, and turned her to face the ancient gilt mirror on a wall between two cabinets.

Her gasp of wonder was soundless. Never had she seen anything so delicately and magnificently lovely. The large central emerald sat over her third eye like a green flower surrounded with delicate diamond leaves, and on each side little florets were sprinkled across her forehead and hair. It was completely beautiful, and it made her almost beautiful, giving to her eyes a depth of colour they seldom had, making her seem mysterious, almost other-worldly.

"This was my mother's favourite jewel," Prince Karim told her softly, his voice coming from a curious distance. "My father allowed her to choose from any jewel in his treasury when I was born."

His face appeared behind her in the mirror, his darkness a strange, almost fairy-tale contrast to her pale gold. She looked into the reflection of his compelling black eyes, and was caught. Slowly his hands tightened on her shoulders, and she watched helplessly as his gaze left her reflection and fell on her, with an expression on his face she could not read.

"I give you this jewel, Caroline."

His strong hands ruthlessly turned her towards him, and her gaze had no choice but to meet his eyes directly, nor her lips any choice but to meet his lips. He bent his head, his grip tightening almost painfully on her shoulders, his lips parting as they touched hers. Then he pulled her roughly in against him and she felt pure, raw passion in his hold.

For one terrible, wonderful moment she felt her own desire surge up to meet his, for one wild moment endless possibility was before her again. Then common sense returned, and she jerked herself violently out of his grasp, away from the seductive touch of his arms, chest and thighs. They stood heaving with breath for a few seconds, and her hand came up and she tore the wonderful jewel from her hair.

"No, thank you!" she whispered breathlessly, holding it out to him. "Nothing that has happened gives you the right to assume that I'm for sale. Not even at this price! Though no doubt I should be flattered that it's so high!"

He clenched his jaw, as if biting back some answer, and wordlessly took the jewelled headdress from her. He restored it to its case, and in silence ushered her to the door again. In silence they returned the way they had come, and at last arrived again in the little apartment that was her prison.

The second course of their meal was awaiting them. The banality of it staggered her, and as he led her to the table and they sat, again she wondered if everything that was happening was a deliberate part of a process of manipulation.

At a sudden thought, she frowned. "When did you come

up with this idea, anyway? I mean, you were waiting for me at the airport, with your pretence all in place! How did you know I was coming to the country?''

"It was I who arranged that you should come."

Her eyes stretched wide. "You *arranged* it? What—that I should win…" Her brain rushed ahead of her speech, and she interrupted herself. "You mean the whole raffle thing was a scam?" She began to laugh helplessly. "My God, David was right! He said it was a scam! Isn't that just—! If only I'd listened!" Another gust of laughter swept her.

"Stop laughing, Caroline," he ordered, and just like that, the incipient hysteria died in her. "The raffle was invented with the hope that your fiancé would buy a ticket. When you bought the ticket we assumed that if you won both you and your fiancé would take the prize trip."

"What were you going to do if you got David into your clutches?"

He lifted a hand. "That is not important now. We had to change our plans to suit the changed circumstances. You were here, your fiancé was not. He has my jewel." He looked at her. "Now I have his."

She smiled cynically into his eyes. "It must be really sweet to know you've taken the blush off the bloom, too! The only problem is that David never knew I was a virgin, and Western men nowadays don't place quite the same value on virginity in their wives as they used to. So if I never tell him, he'll never know how complete your revenge was."

"I understand your bitterness, Caroline."

"Oh! Oh, well, that's fine!" she mocked. "Then I don't have to worry my little head about telling you what a complete, utter and total bastard you are!"

"Caroline, I make allowances for your anger. But I will not allow you to speak to me like this. Do not do so again."

She shivered, and rallied. "What's the penalty for insulting the king in these parts? Will you pull out my tongue? Or is it one of those cut-off-the-right-hand offences?"

He gazed at her. In spite of herself she fell silent.

"So what are you going to do now?" she demanded after a pause.

"One of the members of my personal staff is in New York. He has told your fiancé that you are being held here, and asked for the return of Shakur's jewel. When he returns to Barakat with it, you will be released."

"And in the meantime, I'm your prisoner?"

He bowed.

Caroline took a sip of wine and gazed at him. "He won't do it."

"Pardon me?"

"David told me when we got engaged that I should understand that in the event of kidnap he was completely opposed to any ransom being paid. He said that his life wouldn't be worth living if he ever paid a ransom, or had a ransom paid for him." She gazed levelly at him. "He said that if I were kidnapped nothing would induce him to pay a ransom and I should not expect it."

Karim's eyes narrowed and he said something she did not understand. Caroline was half terrified, half triumphant. Now that it was too late, she saw how foolish it was to have told him what she had just told him.

In truth, she couldn't be sure what David would do. If he got her letter breaking the engagement beforehand, she was certain that he would not bow to the ransom demand, but if not? Oh, why had she been so quick to write that letter? And Prince Karim—what would he do if David merely showed the emissary her letter and denied all knowledge of the seal? What did she know of him, after all? Everything he had told her when she knew him as Kaifar was a lie. Perhaps he would put her to a grisly death as a warning to others. *This is what happens to those who steal from kings.*

Anything was possible.

The world was so different, her future so changed from what she had been imagining a couple of hours ago when she awoke from her dream of perfect bliss. Her imagination could not come up with any answers when she tried to look into the future.

Eleven

Caroline switched out the light and then stood waiting for her eyes to acclimatise. When she could by starshine distinguish the shape of the bed, she softly pressed down on the old-fashioned handle and inch by inch drew the door open. Then she stood waiting, listening, the darkness giving welcome acuteness to her hearing. She soundlessly slipped her bare feet over cool tiles and then silk carpet.

Around her neck her sneakers hung tied by their laces. She had no money, no passport, no ticket. She was wearing the diamond solitaire and all her other jewellery. She would use them as money if necessary.

To go up a tree and over the garden wall would be simple if the guard were asleep or she managed to elude him, but she was not confident. The other possibility carried much more risk, but also perhaps more chance of success. Surely no one would be expecting her to try to escape *into* the palace—where Prince Karim had taken her earlier this evening. She was almost certain that when they returned, he had not locked the door.

It took her several agonized minutes to make her way to the corridor in the darkness, but she made quick progress along it to the door at the end.

It opened. She could feel the movement of air as she slipped into the main part of the palace. Here she could see more easily, lights outside giving faint illumination to the vast rooms. She sidestepped pillars and slipped through doorways with a speed that would have been gratifying if only she had known where she was going. She wished she had looked less at the portraits and more at the exits when Prince Karim had been leading her.

The palace had huge windows, a hundred doors—and so many rooms. She was looking for an open window, an unlocked external door. But if she did not get out tonight, Caroline told herself with the optimism that comes with taking action, she would hide out until morning. And then, with luck, she might even be able to walk right out of the place. She could pretend to be a lost tourist.

There were a hundred possibilities, and her heart was full of hope until a door opened, a light went on and, at the far end of the room Prince Karim, barefoot, naked to the waist, his hair tousled with sleep, hunger in his dark eyes, said, "So you found your way."

She turned without a word and began to run. They were at opposite ends of a long room filled with furniture, and she simply ran to the nearest archway and through it. Now she was in a black-and-white-tiled hallway with pillars and doorways, and to the left, a staircase running up beside a huge stained glass window. Her barefoot flight was sound-less as she made for the stairs, and within seconds she was on the next floor. A long wide corridor marked with pillars and arches and with windows to the floor stretched ahead of her, and the gentle breeze told her that a window was open. She found it and ran out onto a balcony, her heart in her mouth—but the balcony overlooked a small internal courtyard. She would gain nothing except a possible sprained ankle if she leapt down here.

She jumped back inside in time to see Karim enter the corridor at the far end. Hoping he had not seen her, she dodged behind a pillar, tore her sneakers from around her neck, threw them further down the long corridor against a table that rattled under the blow, then dashed through a doorway opposite her. Then she found herself running through a succession of doorways and rooms.

She could not risk pausing to listen for pursuit; she just kept running in the hopes of coming to a window facing outward. She couldn't believe the size of the place—there seemed to be an unending succession of rooms in which beds alternated with divans, scarcely recognizable in the shadowy light. Sometimes she bumped into small tables in the gloom, and several times heard the sound of smashing china.

Then at last she heard what she had been praying not to hear—the soft pad of naked feet running close behind her. She tore open another door, and ran through—into a closet. A hoarse cry ripped from her throat as she turned back into the other room.

But he was there now, in the doorway, coming straight at her. Panting with panic, Caroline whirled and tried to dodge, but with a cry of animal triumph he caught her. Almost before she knew it he lifted her and threw her down onto the bed, and then he was on top of her, panting and furious, his body all the length of hers, his hands roughly grasping her.

For a moment they lay staring into each other's faces. And then, his hands clenching almost painfully on her,

Prince Karim bent and ruthlessly clamped his mouth on hers.

She struggled, but her body's writhing only made him press her more tightly, made the pressure of his mouth more ruthless as he sucked her lips and invaded the moist softness of her mouth. His hunter's rage shifted, and then the angry hardness in him was the hardness of sexual demand. She felt its pressure between her legs, felt how thin was the cotton that covered him, felt her own body's answering heat, and cried out her rejection of the melting within her.

Again she writhed and tried to throw him off, but this only parted her thighs and brought his sex more firmly against hers, so that sensation and anticipation slivered through her veins, silencing and stilling her against her will. He lifted his mouth from hers now, and moved his hips hungrily in the soft cradle of hers while he watched her in the darkness. A wash of sensation roared upwards from the place where their bodies met to her head, her breasts, even to her fingertips. Her mouth opened on a soundless gasp as she fought to resist both her desire, and his.

He bent his head, but with a whispered grunt she turned to avoid the dangerous passion of his kiss. He brushed his lips instead over the tender skin under her ear, and felt her shiver. When she swung her head back, he caught her open mouth, and slipped his tongue between her parted lips, hungry, seeking, demanding that response which she was trying to hide from him. She struggled and he caught both her hands and held them above her head, and her own helplessness sent a wild sexual rush through her, as though her deepest femininity craved this expression of his male potency. She bit her lip to hide her melting, overwhelming desire from him.

But now, as though his body, locked like a magnet against that cluster of nerves between her thighs, could read every thrill that ran through her, Prince Karim abruptly thrust her thighs wide apart and began to rub his sex against hers, in the rhythm that only hours ago he had learned would bring her the sweet drunkenness that her body craved.

She could not hide from him what happened then. Pleasure fountained up in her too suddenly, and her hips heaved up against his, desperate not to lose the contact that was the source of such pleasure. He rode and rocked her, and as the sensations subsided in her, his mouth found hers again, and now she felt too drugged to resist. Her body had tasted the cup, and it would drink deeper, however her heart and her head protested that her lover was her enemy.

The thought was enough to give her strength. As Karim lifted himself away from her and his hand found the waistband of her jeans, she pushed him and rolled off the bed, stumbling to her feet. Her breast heaving, she faced him.

He lay on his back, watching her in silence. "No!" she said. "How dare you!"

With narrowed eyes, silent as a cat, he swung to his feet. His hand snapped around her wrist. He said, "Are you such a fool as to wake a man from his dreams in order to say *no?* What were you looking for, if not to be made love to again? What did you want, if not to be chased and taken?"

Caroline gasped. "I was trying to escape from my prison!" she hissed, and realized a second later how foolish she was to have told him. "Have you forgotten I'm here against my will? I don't want you! How dare you imagine that I—"

His eyes glittered in the pale light of the stars coming through the window. With a small jerk on her wrist he pulled her against him. "I do not *imagine,* Caroline. If you in truth do not want me to prove to you how your body seeks pleasure from mine, and finds it there, do not tempt me with challenges. I have in my veins the blood of generations of men who understood how a woman may provoke a man in order to prove his strength.''

Her heart kicked almost painfully behind her ribs and she pulled away to arm's length, but he held her firm. "That's disgusting!"

"It is survival. A woman who submits to a weak man will have weak sons. Therefore she makes an opportunity for a man to prove himself strong before submitting. This is the law of nature. Beware how you stir it in me, and in yourself."

Childishly, she taunted, "I'd rather have weak sons than the unfeeling towers of strength your women will have!"

With curious timeliness, she lifted her hand to brush a lock of hair from her forehead, and David's diamond on her finger glittered for a moment in starlight. Karim released his hold on her other wrist and captured this one, looking down at the ring. "In truth," he said, "if you marry this man, you will have weak sons—if you have any."

"David is six feet tall and works out three times a week!"

He gazed levelly into her eyes. "Your sons by him will be weak in heart, weak in spirit, weak in humanity. In the desert we are taught that a man's physical strength is merely the vessel that holds better strengths."

The contempt that threaded his tone infuriated her. How dare *he* judge David?

"Like, for example, kidnapping a woman for ransom?" Caroline taunted. "Is that part of your magnificent desert code?"

"Caroline, do not use this tone with me. I am also a king. I have an additional code to live by, the code of responsibility for my people. Your fiancé has attacked the peace of Barakat as surely as if he came with an army of tanks and crossed the frontier. Such a man, and all those belonging to him, must beware that what he starts may be finished by others, in ways other than he hoped.''

''You didn't have to pretend interest in me! You didn't have to undermine my whole life! You didn't have to make love to me to protect your people!'' she burst out. ''Why didn't you just snatch me off the street? That would have been easier to take than...than...''

She ran out of words, almost sobbing with rage and a turbulence of other feelings she did not want to name.

His hand still enclosed her wrist. He tightened its hold possessively. ''This was no part of my plan. I pretended nothing for you that I do not feel, Caroline, though it would have been better if I had not felt it. You know that.''

''Do I?''

''If you do not, it is because in your innocence you understand neither my passion, nor your own efforts to arouse it. Therefore, I tell you plainly that you must not do such things as come to my apartments in the night.''

''I did not come to your apartments! I was looking for a way out of this maze of a palace!''

He stood for a moment with bent head, not answering her. ''I will lead you back to the harem,'' he said. ''If you come to me again in the night, Caroline, there will be no protests. I will take you as you wish to be taken, as I wish to take you.''

She shivered all over. Words leapt to her throat, so many that she did not know where to begin. In the end, silence was her answer, and after a moment he turned and, not loosing his hold on her, led her from the room.

Not until they were back in the harem did he put on a light. They had walked in darkness and silence, a silence for Caroline broken only by the thrumming of her confused heart.

In the main room, he guided her to a chair by the table where they had eaten. "Wait there," he said. He disappeared down a corridor and returned a few minutes later with a pot of coffee. She sat watching bemusedly as he found a mat, set the pot on the table in front of her, and then found cups in the beautifully carved and painted cabinet. In Kaifar such actions would have been ordinary. In Prince Karim they seemed remarkable.

He sat opposite her and lifted the coffeepot and his eyebrows in enquiry. She mutely nodded. Karim poured two cups, pushed one to her, drank from his own. Caroline used cream and sugar and then drank deeply. It might keep her awake, but nothing was going to get her to sleep tonight anyway.

"Caroline," he began. "You were trying to escape?"

She raised her chin and stared at him.

"A resourceful woman might perhaps escape from this palace. It is unlikely, but I do not tell you that it is impossible. The more so because my staff are instructed to lay no hand on you, either to help or hinder you. They will not unlock doors for you, but nor will anyone pull you from a wall if you try to climb over it. Instead they will call me, and I will certainly prevent your leaving.

"Caroline, under these circumstances I ask for your word that you will not try to escape until we have concluded negotiations with your fiancé."

She gasped and laughed with shock. "Are you crazy? I might be able to escape, so please will I promise not to try?"

He was calm in the face of her mockery. "Caroline, you have not understood me. Kidnapping is a crime in West Barakat. I only, of all the citizens of this country, am above the law. A king may break the law for the good of the country, but he should not, except in extreme cases, ask any citizen to break the law for him. That is why I kidnapped you in the way that I did—so that no accomplices would be necessary. Only a very few individuals know that you are here against your will. Those around you here do not know, and they speak no English. They are loyal to me, however, and it is unlikely—even if you could make yourself understood—that they would aid your escape if they discovered it.''

He was too imposing a presence like this, his powerful chest and arms bare and glowing golden in the soft light, the curvature of the muscles both beautiful and firmly male, the musky midnight smell of his skin reminding her of the touch of him, the neat mat of hair on his chest trailing in a line down the centre of his stomach and disappearing under the low waist of his flowing white cotton pants, and his eyes and the movement of his mouth hypnotic as he talked.

"Why are you telling me all this?" she demanded.

"Because, Caroline, if the guard were to find you stumbling around the palace or the grounds in the way that I did tonight, he would kindly, imagining it to be your destination, lead you to my bedroom. And we know now what happens when you come to me in the night.''

Her spine jerked her upright as if electricity had shot through her. "How dare you!" she exploded furiously. "What kind of threat is that?"

He calmly shook his head. "It is not a threat, Caroline. You know very well that your body and mind are at war about me. You are angry because I betrayed your trust, but you are more angry with yourself because your body has experienced no betrayal. Between our bodies, at least, the promise you heard was kept.''

He leaned forward and stroked her cheek and she closed her eyes. "Your body wants more, as it should, and it trusts me to give what it wants, as it should. I explain all these things to you because you were a virgin. Such explanations would not have been necessary for an experienced woman. But you—your body may lead you where you afterwards bitterly resent having gone if you are not warned, or if you do not heed the warning."

"Believe me, my body wouldn't lead me to you if you were the last man on earth!" she exclaimed childishly.

His eyes pierced her with a black hunger that reached down deep inside her and caused her womb to clench with anticipation. "Caroline, I am a man of experience. The physical bond between us is of great power. Do not through ignorance underestimate this power. You must be on your guard against yourself."

"Oh, and you don't have to be, I suppose!"

He half smiled at her. "Have I not made it clear? I am on my guard every minute with you, Caroline. I do not sit one moment in your company without wanting you, I do not lie in my bed at night without dreaming of you, of how you would respond if I came to you and touched you...even now, my heart, my body—my blood promises me that if I caressed you, Caroline, if I kissed you, you could not resist."

She swallowed convulsively, wrestling with the urge to challenge him in the very way he warned her not to—to hit him, or to get up and run, knowing there was nowhere to go, to provoke his desire to a pitch that neither of them could resist. She retreated behind denial.

"You may know what it's like for you, but you have no way *at all* of knowing that this is anything special for me, Karim. For anything you know to the contrary, I could be like this with every man on two legs."

He was half smiling still, shaking his head through most of this speech. "What?" she demanded resentfully.

"Caroline, it is so simple—if you had felt this passion for others, I would not have found you a virgin yesterday."

She slapped him. Panic, rage, desire, pain and the pent-up need for a physical expression of her feelings for him all contributed to her abrupt loss of control, and she slapped him with all her might across his hard brown cheek.

Twelve

He caught her wrist. The coffee cups rattled, and then there was silence and they were frozen, her hand held high in his, gazing at each other while Caroline's heart seemed to discover a new rhythm.

It was her left hand, and after a moment, as if distracted by the flash, he tilted his grip with slow deliberation and his eyes moved to look again at the diamond on her finger. She saw his jaw tighten, and now when his gaze found hers again it was hard. "You will marry this man in spite of what I have told you about him, in spite of all that you have learned of his character?"

To tell him the truth would be to admit to him how deep it had gone with her. It was all she had left, not to let him know that while he had been plotting to kidnap her, she had been falling in love. Caroline glared at him.

"Isn't that what 'for better or for worse' means? Anyway, how do I know David stole your jewel? Why should

I take *your* word for it?'' she demanded. ''It hasn't been good for much so far!''

He ignored the gibe. ''In truth, you are not a sacrifice on the altar of daughterly love. If you sacrifice everything for the sake of wealth, it is for your own sake, not your parents'. You wish to be a wealthy man's wife.''

She snatched her hand from his hold. ''You know nothing about me. And you know even less about honour. So please don't take the high moral ground with me, Kaifar, or Prince Karim, or whoever you may be!''

The flash of his eyes was harder than the diamond's. ''I am both Kaifar and Karim,'' he informed her.

''Kaifar is your middle name so you weren't really lying?'' she mocked.

''In a manner of speaking, Kaifar is my name. It means retribution. I will bring retribution on your fiancé.''

She shivered at the sound of his voice. For David's sake as well as her own she hoped that he would give in to the ransom demand. ''So what does that mean? You didn't lie to me?''

''Is it beyond your comprehension that some things must be more important than the personal, Caroline?'' he responded with angry intensity. ''Can you not understand that my duties as ruler of my country come before anything else? Do you really tell me that to lie to you about my name and occupation was worse than to let a country fall into civil war, to leave it open to attack?''

She dropped her eyes and did not answer.

''Answer me,'' he commanded.

How could she say that it was not the lie about his name that had destroyed her, but the lie about who he was? She could not admit to him that she had dreamed—she had hardly admitted it to herself—dreamed that Kaifar did not know his own heart, that he would find, in the end, that he loved her. Only when he had blasted the dream to dust had she even recognized what her hopes had been. She had hoped that he would want to marry her, she had dreamed of making his country her home…

"I just don't think you have the right to judge me for what I'm doing. Or judge David either," she said.

He shook his head and lifted his coffee cup, bending his head to take a drink. When he had drained the cup he looked at her again. His voice when he spoke was without emotion, resigned.

"Whatever you think about the rights and wrongs, you now understand what I mean to do. You have had time to think. I ask you again whether you will give me your word not to try to escape until I have the jewel seal in my possession. What do you answer?"

Caroline heard exasperation and fatigue in his tone, and her heart contracted. She felt the deep urge to reassure him, to tell him that she was on his side and would help him get the jewel back. As she opened her mouth, she suddenly saw what was going on. Even now he could manipulate her. Even now she loved him, wanted to make the sacrifices that love would make! She couldn't believe that hate and love could exist side by side like this! Or that one part of her could so ignore the truth of what he had done, how little she meant to him! Was she some kind of masochist? Help him get his jewel back, and then without a backward glance he would send her back to David?

She waited till he looked at her. Then she said levelly, "You can count on me as much as I could count on you, Your Highness. If I were you, I wouldn't trust me out of your sight."

He nodded as if this response were no more than he had expected, and rubbed his eyes. Setting his coffee cup down, he stood. "I understand," he said. "Perhaps you would like to go back to bed now. It is very late."

"Don't tell me what to do!" she flared.

"I do tell you what to do," he informed her. "Have you forgotten that you are my prisoner here? Go to your room. If you do not sleep, that is your own choice, but the other choice you do not have."

"What will you do if I don't?" she challenged.

"Caroline, we have had this discussion. If you do not go to your bedroom under your own steam, I will pick you up and carry you there. But then you must face the possibility that I will not immediately leave. If you allow me to carry you to your bed, you must expect me to stay. Now choose wisely."

Trying to disguise the bolt of sheer sexual excitement that shot through her at his words, she got hurriedly to her feet. Feigning an indignation she didn't feel, she stomped off and opened the bedroom door. When she turned to speak, he was a few yards behind her with a cushion in his hand.

"What are you going to do with that?" she demanded.

Karim raised his eyebrows. "I am going to use it as my pillow, since you will not allow me to lie on your breasts. Or between your thighs." He saw his words strike her, and a dark smile appeared in his eyes. "Or perhaps you will change your mind, Caroline. Perhaps you are remembering that to have me between your thighs was a pleasure."

She wanted to shout at him, but the words caught in her throat. "You're not sleeping in here!" she managed finally, as he approached closer and closer.

Karim smiled and dropped the cushion onto the floor. "Not until you invite me, Caroline," he said softly. "Meanwhile I sleep across the threshold."

"Are you crazy?" she shrieked.

He took no notice of the exclamation. "Go inside and close the door. Do not come out again until morning."

"You can't sleep on the floor!"

He let out a crack of laughter. "Why not?"

"It's not comfortable! You won't get any sleep!"

"If I do not, it will not be because the floor is not comfortable," he said. His voice sent a thrill of excitement through her. "You do not go in and close your door, Caroline. Is it because you wish after all to invite me into your bed?"

She was gazing at him like a hypnotized rabbit, or whatever it was that got hypnotized by two bright beams of light. Only she was hypnotized, too, by the half-smiling mouth, the strong, beautiful body, brown and muscled, the thighs under the thin cotton, the sexual intensity of his being. The memory of what all those things meant rippled through her body and her mind. With an effort Caroline tore her eyes away.

"Sleep on the floor, then!" she snapped childishly. "I don't care if you're uncomfortable!"

"Why should you?" he agreed. He sank down lightly into a squatting position, knees apart, rocking on his toes, smiling up at her, and spoke seductively. "If you do not want to invite me into your bed, you could sleep here, on top of me. My body is softer than the floor."

"Not by much!" she cried, and instantly blushed. Of course she hadn't meant that, she had meant to insult him with his inhumanness, but even she heard a different meaning in the words she had spoken.

"Ah, Caroline, how you flatter a man! My body stirs to hear this on your lips."

In truth, she had been astonished at the marble hardness of his sex yesterday. She had known the mechanics of the sexual act, everyone did; she knew that when a man was

sexually excited he grew hard...but that human flesh could
be so completely unlike flesh, as hard as he had been, she
hadn't imagined. She remembered her own wanton admi-
ration of him in the wild heat of the night, remembered
what she had done, what he had done, and blushed with a
mixture of desire and embarrassment,

Her eyes drifted to that area covered by his pyjama bottoms but now visibly straining against the fabric, and her
own body melted to think that a few unguarded words from
her had made him respond. If she said the word, he would
do to her again what he had done yesterday...pleasure beyond anything she had imagined or dreamed or even hoped
sex was.

He caught her hand in one of his, and sank down into a
sitting position on the floor, stretching his legs out and
drawing her down after him. Even that touch of his skin
on hers made her shiver with anticipation. He pulled her
until she was bent over him, then slipped his other hand
around her neck and drew her mouth towards his.

Electricity shot through all her nerves, and her mouth
parted involuntarily to invite his kiss. Then, exerting the
last of her resistance, Caroline jerked upright.

"Leave me alone!" she cried. If she let him make love
to her again, knowing what she now knew, she was a fool.
He would addict her to pleasure, she was sure of it. But
when he had his jewel back, whatever he said about his
desire for her, she knew without being told that he would
send her home. She did not want to feel any more desperate
than she felt now, but if she let him make love to her again
and again...she would end up begging him not to let her
go.

She was already a prisoner in the ancient harem. Did she
want to be a concubine of the Prince of West Barakat?

"Leave me alone!" she cried again, pulled her hand out of his, and drew back inside the bedroom.

"Lock the door," Prince Karim commanded softly, before stretching his long, strong body across her doorway.

"I don't think you understand my client's position," the lawyer said.

Three men—David Percy, his lawyer and Nasir—were sitting in a large, spacious office high over New York. The lawyer was behind a massive desk, with David sitting to one side of it. Both men were facing Nasir. Behind them, Nasir could see, if he looked, all the economic and political power of New York spread out beyond the glass.

"My client is not in possession of the Jewel Seal of Shakur, has never been in possession of it, and therefore is not in a position to supply it to your employer."

"Forgive me, Mr. Standish, but I am afraid it is you who do not fully appreciate your client's position. The Jewel Seal of Shakur is certainly in his possession at this moment, and just as certainly it did not come there honestly. We have information and evidence to that effect. Therefore your client should think carefully before taking any intransigent stand."

"We are not taking a stand. We merely inform you, and through you the Prince of West Barakat, that we are unable to comply with his demand. He should release Ms. Langley from confinement immediately if he wishes to prevent my client or her parents from going to the police."

Nasir looked grave but made no reply.

"I think we should point out to your employer that Americans take a dim view of American citizens being taken hostage on foreign soil, and if your little kingdom wishes to continue friendly relations with the American government and benefit from lucrative American tourism, he should do everything in his power to restore Ms. Langley to her family without delay," David interjected.

"If this story were to get into the press—that the prince himself has taken a hostage in a bid for gain—you can rest assured that American tourists would not be eager to visit the country."

The lawyer frowned, and David fell silent.

"In particular we remind you that the United States was one of the signatories to the very favourable trade agreement signed by the Barakat Emirates only a few years ago. No doubt Prince Karim will wish to consider all the ramifications before he takes this ridiculous situation any further."

There was a silence when the lawyer finished speaking. Nasir looked sadly from one man to the other. "And is this your final position on the matter, Mr. Percy?" he asked.

The lawyer answered for him. "It is. In the circumstances, there could not be any other."

Nasir nodded, his eyes still sorrowful, and got to his feet. "I am very sorry to hear that, gentlemen. Very sorry indeed. I know His Serene Highness Prince Karim will also be very sad when he hears this news. I have already advised you most strenuously not to make this public, either with the police or with the press. I shall not repeat myself. Good day to you."

Thirteen

She awoke late and lay looking slowly around her prison. She felt depressed and tired in a way she didn't think she'd ever felt in her life, as if during the night the truth of her situation had filtered through the layers of her being, and now weighed her down everywhere.

First her father hadn't loved her, then her fiancé; and now a man whom she had really believed understood and accepted her as she was had merely been calculating every move in order to kidnap her without fuss. This final blow seemed worst. It seemed to cut at the deepest layers of her sense of self.

Was she so unlovable? Would there never be someone who loved her, Caroline Langley, for herself?

She could hear music playing somewhere, the kind of wailing Barakati music she had imagined she would learn to love. But no one would ask her to learn to love it now. Hostage to Prince Karim. How foolish her dreaming seemed in the cold light of reality. As Kaifar he had warned her. Why hadn't she listened?

She sighed. Thinking would get her nowhere. Caroline got up and took a cool shower, then, hoping she would be allowed to walk in the garden, dressed in a full-skirted cotton sundress in white with bold splashes of purple and green. She put on no shoes, because she liked the cool feel of the marble tiles under her feet. When she came out to the main room, to her surprise Karim was there with another man, sitting at the table.

"Good morning, Caroline," said Karim.

"Good morning, Your Highness" she returned.

"This is my brother. Rafi, meet Caroline."

"Hi, Caroline." Rafi stuck out a hand which she ignored.

"How do you do, Your Serene Highness? What an honour it is to meet another member of this noble family," Caroline said, dropping a curtsey.

Karim looked at her, and in spite of herself, she fell silent.

"Come and sit down, Caroline," he said.

She took the chair at the end of the table and sat facing the two men. They regarded her gravely for a long moment, and at last she said with impatient anxiety, "What is it?"

"David Percy has refused our offer," said Karim. "He will not give up the jewel."

Caroline closed her eyes, and a wave of misery and fear washed over her. It was one thing for David to warn her, one thing for her to say to Karim that it would be so. It was something very different to hear it confirmed. She was not worth even that in David's eyes. He would not even restore a stolen object to its owner to save her life. Worse— to save her from imprisonment and unknown cruelties. It was deeply, darkly depressing.

But she wouldn't let Karim see that. She forced her eyes

to open and gazed at him, disguising her feelings as best she could. "I told you he wouldn't," she said roughly. But she found she couldn't look at him. Her gaze dropped to her hands in her lap. She concentrated on interlacing her fingers as if it were a delicate, difficult task.

"What are you going to do now?" She swallowed, and found the strength to look at the two men. "Send him a piece of me?"

She started to shake. What would they do to her? What hope was there for her? She was in the hands of the highest power in the land. Who would ask questions of the king? Who would come after her? She looked at the two men in front of her. They could do whatever they wanted. She had no hope.

The world seemed to turn grey. The next thing she knew, Prince Rafi was pressing a cup of steaming coffee into her hand. Gratefully she sipped it. It was strong and black, and it steadied her.

"Caroline, we mean you no personal harm," Rafi said. "You will not be hurt while you are kept here."

"Keeping me here is hurting me," she said dully. Karim, she noticed, said nothing, merely sat looking at her with his desert brigand's face, hard and unforgiving. She wondered if the coffee was drugged, and then, realizing it made no difference, shrugged and drank again.

"We would like to approach your father," Karim said. "To ask your father to intervene with David Percy. If this does not work, we shall seek other means. What is your opinion, Caroline, of your father's probable influence with this man?"

"You're taking for granted that my father would want to use his influence?"

Rafi threw a startled look between his brother and Caroline.

"Of course," said Karim.

"Well, forgive my astonishment, but only a few days ago you were hammering home the truth that my parents didn't love me!" she said bitterly, and then wished she hadn't, because it made her want to cry when she should be strong. "Or was that only so that you would seem like my only port in a storm?"

"There are not so many men like David Percy in the world," Karim told her roughly. "Your father perhaps loved his other children more than you, but if he were capable of not wishing to help you now, he would be not merely selfish, but a monster."

"We would like you to talk to your father on the telephone, to reassure him that you are well, and ask him to exert pressure on your fiancé. Will you do this?" Rafi added.

It was astonishing how much his words suddenly made her long to hear her father's voice. She felt as if she were going crazy, torn from every comfortable and familiar landmark. She needed something familiar to remind her who she was. Her father's voice would—had to!—put her on an even keel again.

"Yes," she said, unable to disguise the eagerness she felt. "I'm sure if he knew what David was doing—yes, I'll talk to him!"

Karim spoke. "One thing, Caroline—you must not divulge exactly where you are. If you do so, we will be forced to move you to another location. It will not be so comfortable as the palace."

"All right, all right, I promise!" Caroline replied.

The phone was already there, a pre-war black dial phone with a curved receiver and ivory and gold fittings that looked as though it had been made to last forever and was doing so. Caroline was almost sure that there had been no phone in this room before. Had it been locked in a cupboard? She would keep her eyes open when it was put away.

Karim dialled, spoke to someone, waited, and then held the receiver between them so that he could hear.

"Hello?"

It was her father's voice, and Caroline started to cry. "Dad?" she sobbed. "Dad, is that you?"

"Caroline!" he shouted in disbelief. "*Caroline?* Where are you?"

"I'm in Barakat," she began, as Karim lifted his finger in warning. "I can't tell you exactly. Dad, has—David told you what happened?"

"It wasn't David who broke the news. It was a journalist. We've been trying to get news all day. Is it true? Caroline, what's happening? Have you escaped?"

"I haven't escaped. I've been told to make this call. Dad, but have you talked to David? They want to know if you've talked to him," she said in response to a mouthed instruction from Karim. His mouth was so close to hers, the perfume of him was in her nostrils, but this morning it was the scent of betrayal she smelled. Her heart beat fast, but with stress and misery, not with excitement.

It took only a few sentences to get across the message the princes wanted delivered. Talk to David. Urge him to cooperate and return the jewel.

After a short silence, her father said quietly, "He denies having anything to do with the stone, Caroline. He says this is some kind of tactic."

"Prince Karim says he has proof."

"Proof that David stole his jewel?" He sounded shocked.

"Yes."

"You've talked to the prince himself?"

If you only knew. "Yes, I've talked to him. Dad, they're going to hang up now. Will you tell David?"

"I'll tell him, sweetheart. And if he has that jewel you better believe he's going to give it back. You sit tight, we'll get you out of there," said her father, and then the connection was cut.

Caroline burst into sobs. It was the first time in her life her father had ever called her sweetheart.

Karim put down the receiver and spoke over her head to Rafi. "Her father was called by a journalist."

Rafi swore and got to his feet. "When?"

Karim only shook his head. "I'll report back," said Rafi, and ran lightly down the corridor that led to the main part of the palace.

Caroline sobbed herself into silence and then was aware of Karim's silence beside her.

"Take off the ring," he commanded.

She sniffed and wiped her face with the back of her hand, staring at him uncomprehendingly over it. "What?"

"Take off his ring. Do you consider yourself engaged to a man such as this? It is obscene. You abase yourself with such an alliance." His voice was harsh, his eyes pinpoints of black light, his jaw set. She thought, *I hope David knows what he's doing, crossing a man like this.*

But she wasn't going to let that fear show. "I told you he wouldn't," she said, half triumphantly.

"You told me, and I did not believe it. Can there be such a man in the world? After this, how can you believe that he loves you in any way, Caroline? He is without even respect for your humanity. Take off the ring."

"It's a question of principle," she said, not believing it, but holding it up against herself like a shield. "If he once paid a ransom, he'd be vulnerable, and anyway, he says that if everyone refused to pay ransoms, there wouldn't be any kidnapping.''

Karim laughed. ''It amuses me to hear that David Percy talks about principles!'' He sobered. ''This is nothing but a disguise for selfishness and lack of love.''

She clasped her right hand protectively over the diamond. ''I know he doesn't love me. I've always known.'' Well, almost. She smiled in bright mockery, though it cost her. ''I guess your research wasn't quite good enough, Your Highness! If you really wanted to hurt David you should have stolen one of his inanimate prize pieces. Then you might have had a deal.''

Prince Karim stared. ''You *know* it? You know that your fiancé does not love you? Why then does he pay your father so much for you? For what can he want you if not love?''

In spite of herself, that caught at her. *For what can he want you, if not love?* Once she had thought that was why Kaifar wanted her. Her heart beating faster, she dropped her head and muttered, ''He wants me because I look like a statue of Alexander the Great.''

Karim's eyes narrowed in astonished incredulity. *''What?''* he whispered with such incredulous ferocity it seemed like anger.

''It's in a museum. It's his favourite bust of Alexander. He's tried to get the museum to give it to him lots of times, offering them huge endowments for it, but they won't.''

''He buys a flesh and blood woman to take the place of a marble statue?'' She had never heard any voice sound so contemptuous. ''And you allow this? For money?''

''You already know all this, Your Highness.''

''Will you stop calling me Your Highness! I am Karim and you may use my name!'' he exploded with regal fury.

She was nervous of him when he was angry, and did not

dare to challenge him, though inwardly she railed at her own cowardice. She did not answer.

"That you do not love him I knew. Of course I knew this after the way you were with me," he continued, and her blood boiled with sudden heat at his meaning. "I did not guess—how could I?—that he did not love you."

She tossed her head to get a curl out of her eye and gazed at him wordlessly.

He returned the look with a deep searching in his gaze that made her shift uneasily in her chair. "And nevertheless you will marry him," he said with dry anger. "You will ally yourself to such a man—a man who has scarcely the right to be called human—you will let him take whatever pleasures he is capable of from your soul and your body, Caroline, giving you none, you will bear his children if he is enough of a man to give you children...you will do this?"

She looked down at the flashing diamond. She didn't want to tell a direct lie, and yet to tell him the truth would leave her so open. If he knew she had broken her engagement for his sake... Karim wanted her. He had told her, and anyway it was in his eyes. But if she gave in to his passion, when that was all it was, what would she have when it was over? And if it was his intention to hurt her if David did not return the seal—how much ammunition such an admission would give him! He would have terrible power over her.

"It's my life, Karim," she said harshly. "What I do with it is none of your business."

Suddenly he cracked with laughter. "It is perverse! That one should buy a statue because it reminds him of a woman he cannot possess—this a man can understand! That he should buy a beautiful, sexual, spirited woman because she reminds him of a statue! This is impossible!'' He laughed loud and shook his head.

Then suddenly he lifted one strong hand and caught her chin, making her look at him. ''Caroline, take what pleasure I offer you.'' His eyes had changed, and she shivered at what passionate, urgent desire she saw in them. ''A man like this will kill your sensual nature, Caroline, and your spirit, very soon. Then you will enjoy nothing anymore. Every man's touch will disgust you.''

He leaned forward, and his voice became deep and urgent with seduction, and she felt excitement whisper along her skin to every sensitive part of her. ''Let me teach you more delights, beloved, before you go to this fate. Between you and me a lifetime would not be long enough for us to taste them all, but I will give you a sampling of what you are so hungry for.

''Caroline, let me do this. Say that you will let me do it.''

Fourteen

Caroline jumped to her feet, and without comment, Karim slowly followed. He stood close, watching her face, as if waiting for her answer.

She had a deep, overwhelming, frightening urge to stretch her arms up around his neck, to feel his arms around her, to weep out all the grief of the world against his chest. She didn't understand how she could feel like this. It was his betrayal that made her want to weep. Why should she seek his comfort for it? Her confusion frightened her.

When he lifted his hand to her chin again, she slapped it and turned away. "Caroline?" he breathed.

"Keep away from me!"

His jaw clenched and his eyes flashed black fire, but he did not touch her again. "Tell me why."

"You know why. You already know," she said, stifling the tears that seemed to want to force their way.

"No," Karim breathed softly. "No, Caroline, I do not

know why. You must tell me a reason. Am I mistaken? I did not give you the pleasure I thought I gave you?''

She swallowed and tossed a lock of hair out of her eyes, fixing him with a stony look, her jaw firmly clenched.

''If this is the case, Caroline, then I ask for another chance. If you were disappointed, perhaps that is because you were a virgin. But your body will learn to trust and take pleasure from the touch of mine, that I know.''

She shook her head in an abrupt negative, biting her lip.

''No?'' he pressed quietly.

''Never *trust*, Karim!'' She looked at him again, her eyes hot with blame. ''Whatever pleasure you gave me, and I don't deny that you did, my body will never trust yours because I can never again trust you!''

She didn't want to be telling him this, she did not want a conversation on the subject, but she couldn't seem to stop the angry flow of words.

''Why not, Caroline?''

''Because you used me, and what I felt for you. Because you pretended desire when all you wanted was a hostage! Why not, you ask? Because I was *betrayed* by you, that's why not!''

''Caroline, this is not what happened.'' He caught her hand, brought it to his lips and dropped a gentle kiss in the palm. He led her to a sofa and made her sit. ''I never pretended desire for you. I always desired you. This I hoped to control. It was not my intention to make love to you. Not then, when I was planning to take you hostage.''

She laughed, then pulled a hankie out of her pocket and wiped her eyes and nose, because the laughter brought the tears dangerously close. ''You had it in mind from the beginning. You came to the airport just for that purpose!''

''No.'' He spoke firmly, frowning a little. ''Recollect

that Rafi and I came to the airport to pick up both you and David Percy. How then could I have had such intentions?''

"And as soon as you saw that your prey had had the sense to elude your trap, you settled on me! Do you deny it?''

"I settled on you, yes. I said, I will take his jewel and force him to give me mine." His eyes burned with the passion of that moment, and she shivered. "The other was no part of my plan, however. The fact that I desired you—" his eyes ruthlessly found hers and gazed into her depths "—as I have desired no other woman...*that* I did not look for. Then my motives became confused. I said to myself that it would be better this way. I could bring you here and share days and nights of love with you so that you would never know that you had been a hostage.''

"Until it was all over, of course!" she said.

"When you came back here with me, Caroline, I awoke from such stupid confusion and knew that I must not take you under such circumstances, even to save you from the pain of knowing you were my hostage. I would have left you, I was determined not to take advantage of you, but— you know what you did to make my leaving impossible.''

It was true. She had begged him to stay, to make love with her. She had even bought the condoms. She whispered, "You weren't—leaving me to get condoms, the way I thought?''

"No, Caroline, I was leaving to save you from me. From my overwhelming desire to make love to you. I would have left you. But it was not to be. You were too beautiful, and you pleaded so sweetly, and—I did not know that you were so completely inexperienced. And so I made you mine. The sweetest of experiences, Caroline.''

"Was it?" she asked bitterly.

She was crying openly, without knowing why. His arms

went around her and drew her against his chest, and she gave in and began to sob. He held her while she cried, and loosed her when she hunted for her hankie again.

And then, when she had dried her cheeks, he bent and his lips, tenderly, sweetly, brushed hers, sending a whisper of electricity through her.

A door banged, and there were running footsteps, and a voice. Karim loosed his hold on her and stood up, just as Rafi burst into the room.

"The damned story is already on the news network!" he called to his brother.

He ran past them, through a broad archway into the room beyond, and through a door off it. Karim followed him, and after a moment, Caroline followed them both.

In this room, one of many where she had never been, was a television set. Rafi had already flicked it on and was channel hopping with the remote. When he got to a talking head, he stopped.

"...a spokesperson at the Consulate of the Barakat Emirates, in Washington, said tonight that they were investigating the allegations. More on that story from our correspondent."

The two princes looked at each other.

"Is that bad news?" Caroline asked.

"It is not something we hoped for," Karim admitted.

"Maybe," Rafi said simultaneously. He lifted the remote and increased the volume as a scene she recognized as some ruins in the dust-blown desert appeared on the screen.

"The Barakat Emirates," the reporter's voice intoned. "Three small kingdoms united by a common currency and a Supreme Parliament..."

They listened in silence. The only news obtainable from Barakat was that Ms. Caroline Langley had entered the country and had not so far left it. As far as anyone at the consulate knew, the Great Jewel Seal of Shakur was not missing, and was still in its rightful place in the treasury of His Serene Highness Sayed Hajji Karim ibn Daud ibn Hassan al Quraishi, Prince of West Barakat and Guardian of the Seal.

Then David's face was on the screen, pretending to a reluctance that she instinctively knew was false. He had probably engineered the interview, but was making it look as though he'd been caught out by a leak. Yes, he had been told that his fiancée was a hostage of Prince Karim himself. He did not want to say much for fear of repercussions. It was not in his power to restore the allegedly missing jewel, since he had never laid eyes on it in his life, and he had so informed the emissary. The emissary had shown no disposition to accept his word.

However, in any case he would not negotiate with kidnappers nor pay any ransom demand. If more people had the courage not to pay ransom, there would be less kidnapping. His staff were under instructions not to pay any ransom if he himself were kidnapped. He had explained his position to his fiancée and she was in full agreement with him.

Caroline had never seen David look so cold as he did in that interview. Far from looking like a distraught fiancé, he showed no emotion whatsoever, not even what an ordinary person would show for a stranger in Caroline's situation. "Naturally I and the family are devastated and hope that she will be released," he said, but he was mouthing the words. She looked down at her ring and thought that if she got out of this with a whole skin, she would always be grateful to Karim for the fact that she had broken her engagement before it was too late.

When it was over, both the princes sat shocked and silent.

"Why is it so bad?" she asked at last.

Karim looked at her. "Do you remember the other day, as we passed a desert village, that I pointed out to you the satellite on the roof of the chief's house?" She nodded.

"Within a day or two, perhaps much less, most of the citizens of Barakat will know that the Seal of Shakur has been stolen and is no longer in the possession of the ruling house. Ordinary citizens will expect bad luck of every kind to follow an announcement like this, and out of their fears will probably create it. But worse than this, my brother Omar has already had trouble with one of the desert sheikhs. This will give the man renewed courage. Other tribes may join him. Then the bad luck which the people expect will indeed happen."

Caroline did not notice that she had begun to feel Karim's problems as her own. She only felt that it would be dreadful if David's selfish greed started a war in this exotic and beautiful place. "Oh, God!" she whispered. "Can't you do something?"

"We *must* do something," said Karim.

Rafi explained, "We didn't take this possibility enough into account. In our original plan, Mr. Percy would not have been free to go to the press. Perhaps later we did not adequately consider the risks." He glanced ruefully at Karim, because it was Rafi, hot-headed as ever, who had urged the kidnapping of Caroline. "We thought the threats would keep him quiet."

Karim called something abrupt in Arabic, and Rafi turned to him, shrugged and muttered an obvious apology.

Caroline stood looking from one to the other as his words sank in. "What did you threaten him with?" she asked slowly. Shivers were running over her skin, though the room was not cold.

Karim had on his familiar stone face. Rafi shrugged uncomfortably. Neither answered.

"What?" she prodded.

"Well," she offered brightly, when it was clear she would get no answer, "there's only one thing kidnappers threaten to do, isn't there? You threatened to kill me." She was curiously cold now, emotionally and physically, and seemed to be above herself somewhere, floating over all their heads. Her voice was high and light, completely disconnected from her emotions. Rafi muttered what sounded like another apology and got up and left.

"Did you mean it?" she asked Karim in that distant tone, as if it were a meaningless social question.

At last Karim spoke. "Of course I have no intention of hurting you in any way, Caroline! We threatened your fiancé because of the reasons I have already told you—to prevent the information getting out to the tribes."

He spoke impatiently, as if to a friend, someone who would naturally believe him and trust him, someone he liked. Was it a front? Was that how it was done? Maybe she would find herself adopting his cause, worried about the risks of an uprising as much as Karim himself was.

"It is not from me that you are in danger, but from your own fiancé! What terrible marriage will you have with this man?"

Caroline stared at him, treacherously beginning to believe him, desperately wanting it to be the truth. How ill-prepared her mind was for resisting this kind of assault, if that was what it was! Why didn't they teach kids this in schools, how quickly the brain started siding with the enemy?

She must not listen to him. She could not afford to, if it meant she stopped trying to escape or relaxed her guard.

"*He* does not know that I will not hurt you! Yet he leaves you to my mercies. Take off his ring!"

As if he had not spoken, she said, "But you wouldn't kill me anyway, not right away. You'll never get your jewel if you do that! No, you have to keep me alive in order to supply the body parts you'll be sending my mother and father, won't you?"

Karim snorted angrily and looked at her from under his brows. He stood up and approached her.

"Don't be such a fool!" he growled.

But she was in full flow. "What will you start with—an ear? That's always a popular item, I understand," she carolled in bitter mockery, indicating her ear as if it were part of some ludicrous fashion display.

"Caroline, stop this!"

"Or a little finger?" Her voice was hoarse now, deep and uncomfortable in her throat, loaded with too much feeling. "The little finger on my right hand? But then, that wouldn't incapacitate me as much as you might like, because I'm left-handed. So maybe it had better be the little finger on the left!"

Angry, tearful, half crazy, hardly knowing what she said, Caroline thrust her hand at him as he stopped before her.

"Why don't you take it now, Karim! You don't want to let David get away with that interview, do you? He might think he'd won!"

With an oath, goaded beyond endurance, Karim caught the hand she offered and lifted his other hand to drag the diamond solitaire off her finger, flinging it furiously away. Her mouth parted in soundless surprise, Caroline heard it clink against marble.

"What—?"

But he gave her no chance to speak. As if this act had destroyed all his self-control, he pulled her roughly against him, her body flat along the length of his, wrapped his arm around her, pushed his other hand into her tangled hair, and ruthlessly, passionately, irresistibly, smothered her mouth with his kiss.

Fifteen

Sensual joy flared into life in her. Her hungry blood surged to meet his body wherever it met hers—in breasts, lips, thighs. She suddenly desperately wanted, *needed,* his touch, his wild caresses, his passionate lovemaking.

His fingers pressed her scalp, holding her mouth against his as if afraid she would escape him. His other arm was hard and unrelenting across her back, her waist, his hand clenched on her hip. His sensual, seeking mouth was ruthless against the softness of hers, sending shock waves of desire flooding through her.

He was hard, and this time she was wearing no heavy denim to keep her body from the full appreciation of his. Two layers of thin cotton were no protection from the knowledge of how much he wanted her, to get inside her, to drown himself in the depths of her.

His hand pressed against the soft flesh of her buttocks, holding her centre there for the thrust of his, the touch melting her. His foot moved between her feet and he bent her back under his kiss, forcing her to spread her legs further, exposing her inner body to his touch. He pressed his sex right against the tenderest part of her flesh.

In spite of his hold, her head fell back, and she gasped for air. "Karim!" she breathed.

His hand in her hair made her look into his blazing dark eyes. "No!" he commanded, "no protests!" and buried his mouth against her throat, her eyelids, and then her mouth again, as if afraid of what he might hear if he let her speak. Her body he was sure of. He kissed her with tender ferocity, his tongue tasting the softness of her full lips, exploring the moist space within, till he had sent electric sensation to every cell of her being, and his own.

His hand released her only to pull up the full skirt of her dress to find the naked skin of her thighs...and the flesh that was covered by thin cotton and lace. His hand pressing against her buttocks and between her legs, his fingers began to stroke against that barrier of lace, and with satisfaction he felt her shuddering response.

Her legs were too far apart for her to offer any resistance as his fingers strayed to the edge of that lace, and gently, teasingly, ran his fingers around it. Her thighs clenched, but she was helpless under the onslaught of so much pleasure; she could not resist. His hand slipped down inside, over her bare rump, and again his fingers stroked her as she melted again and again for him.

Her eyes closed and her mouth soundlessly opened wide as his finger pushed inside her, and with satisfaction he tasted the cry of pleasure on her lips. Soon she would be beyond all protest. His fingers in that moist home of her centre, his palm cupping her to push her body against the full hungry hardness of his, he set up the rhythm as old as time.

Caroline was melting, drowning, filled with electricity and light. His mouth and tongue tasted hers, his hands teased and stroked and burned her with her own yearning desire. She felt his tongue and his fingers take up the same rhythm in her, pushing and sliding against those tender tissues that all damped themselves to ease his passage, encouraging the thrust of tongue and hand and sex.

Excitement, electricity, passion, desire, sensation and melting built to a crescendo in her, and she began to whimper her urgent need for the release that did not come. Arching her back, she drew her upper body away from his, seeking the muscle tension that would allow her release.

He understood, with the direct physical understanding of the body, and released his hold on her. Now his mouth freed her, he turned her body away, and with urgent control he bent her back over one arm while he moved with quick expertise to lift her skirt at the front.

His hand found her again, and now expertly stroked and massaged the moist hungry bud that held the promise of a world of pleasure. Without volition, her legs spread further, inviting his touch, her skin singing, her flesh burning under the fire of his fingers.

That hot, hot centre of burning, with slow delicious tendrils, burst through the universe that was her being, radiating heat and wild pleasure through the dark space of her deepest self.

Caroline sobbed and clung to him as the sweet electricity subsided in her, then felt his muscles tense as he bent to wrap his arm under her knees and, again wildly devouring her mouth with his, lifted her high up in his arms and turned towards the doorway of the luxurious bedroom.

"Now!" he said in triumph, lifting her high. "Now you are mine!"

It was true. She was beyond protest now. She wanted all the pleasure he could give her, and damn tomorrow.

"Is that Mr. Nasir Khan?"

"It is. Who is calling, please?"

"My name is Camille Packer. I'm a freelance writer, and I've been researching a book exposing questionable practices in the antiques trade for the past two years, Mr. Khan."

"Yes?"

"I've been investigating David Percy as part of that book. It's rumoured you have strong evidence that he actually had the Jewel Seal of Shakur copied and then substituted for the real thing. I wonder if you'd be willing to discuss it with me?"

"Ms. Packer, where did you get this information?"

"Mr. Khan, as of half an hour ago, I've been asked to write a piece for the *Times* on this story. I can promise you a very friendly hearing. Can we get together?"

"I will call my employer, Ms. Packer, and ask for instructions."

Karim laid her on the bed and then stood over her, looking down with a mixture of triumph and need in his black eyes, his jaw firm and tight with passionate intent. His eyes locked with hers, he unbuttoned his shirt and threw it impatiently off. When his hands moved to his waist, she closed her eyes and opened her lips on a moan.

"Caroline!" he ordered, and in the cloudy mists she heard him and drunkenly opened her eyes. "Do not close your eyes," he commanded in a quiet hoarse voice. Beside and above her he had pulled apart the waistband of his soft trousers, and was stripping them down his naked hips and buttocks. She saw what he wanted her to see, and her eyelids dropped with too much sensation. She was fainting.

"Caroline!" he said again. He was fully naked now, and she looked at the hard, beautiful body, the curving muscles, the softly brown skin, the black eyes above, and then, involuntarily, her eyes returned to that proud masculine flesh and she smiled and unconsciously licked her lips. "Ah," he breathed, as if that tiny movement had told him something. "Ah, is it so, Caroline?"

She did not understand him, only knew that the sight of him thrilled her, and the knowledge of that excited him. He lifted her dress again and, putting his fingers into the top of her lacy cotton briefs, pulled them all the length of her legs, down over her bare feet, with expert hands.

She lay helpless, drunk, wantonly half naked, willing him to do it, remembering nothing except the pleasure he had given her for the first time in her life, hungry for more. She felt the breath of wind across the skin of her thighs. Then he half lifted, half pushed her further onto the bed, and as he lifted himself towards her, an icicle of fear stabbed through the heat he had made for her, and Caroline made a sudden twist to evade him. How could she still want a man who had—

But she was too late. Even as her thighs closed he was already on top of her, pulling the skirt of her dress higher between them, his naked flesh hot and demanding against hers. He kissed her in silent fury, the fury of sexual need. Her own need smote her like a sword, leaving her gasping.

"Caroline," he begged hoarsely. "Open your legs to me."

She gazed up at him, torn by conflicting needs, by the fear of his potency and of her own response, by the deep desire for the sweet invasion of his body, and by the wish to hurt and deny him what he wanted.

He half smiled, misunderstanding her hesitation. "It will not hurt for long, Caroline," he said, stroking his tongue tantalizingly along her lower lip and then drawing it between his lips and kissing and sucking it so that she felt little tendrils of sensation zing from her mouth to where his body pressed for entry.

"You lied to me, you cheated—you—"

"Open your legs to me, Caroline," he repeated in soft command. "About this I have not lied. I promise you pleasure, and I will give you pleasure."

"I don't want pleasure from you!"

He pressed against her, sending shivers of anticipation through her. "Your body wants mine, my body wants yours, there has never been desire like this," he insisted. "Do not you lie, Caroline. Open your legs. That is the truth between us, that we both want you to open your legs."

"Is that a command, Your Highness?"

He laughed and abandoned speech to flick the tip of his tongue lightly in the folds of her ear, setting up a new pattern of shivering sensation all down her breasts and arm. Then, trailing his tongue across her cheek, he caught her lip and bit it gently between his teeth, and a shock wave of pleasure struck her and left her gasping. She knew that she could not resist her own desire.

But still she tested, still some part of her drove her to punish him.

"Don't," she whispered, as his body pressed urgently against hers, as the sensations trembled through her, fire and ice both at once. The pressure of him, hard against her, and yet with the promise of pleasure in the very hardness...demanding, and yet with a demand that thrilled her through and through—for one crazy instant there flashed through her mind the thought *Does the deer joy in being caught by the tiger even though death is the outcome?*

He watched her eyelids flutter, her head turn in the pillow as sensation assailed her, felt the small hungry movements of her body as it wrestled with the conflicting wishes of her head.

"Caroline, is that what you want? Shall I command you as king to do what you want to do? I command it, then." His hands grasped her wrists and held them above her head. "Open your legs to me, you are mine already," he ordered her.

She burned and melted, and her body convulsed in sexual delight. And in irresistible response to the demands of her body and his, the muscles of her thighs tensed, and drew apart.

He closed his eyes as the emotional and sexual power of this female acceptance swept him up, lifting his head back on his neck, stretching his face into a grimace of triumph and defeat as with one sure thrust he entered the place where he was both master and servant.

She was his. He could make her helpless with the pleasure his body made for her. This act of seeking his pleasure within her made her moan with joy, and the sound of her moans made him hungrier than his system could bear.

He grunted wildly, his body pushing into her over and over, fighting against the pleasure that beckoned him because hearing her cries of passion was an even greater pleasure and he was determined to make her as weak with release as she made him.

Never had he learned so quickly what a woman needed from him, never felt such wild pleasure in giving it to her. He thrust into her over and over, letting his body demand everything, and then, when her cries reached a pitch that he seemed to have known from birth, he pressed down into her and moved against her, like the grinding of pestle and mortar that the old poets spoke of. Then he felt the hot sweet flooding in her that opened her even further, and then as if of its own accord, his body began to thrust again.

He had never experienced such powerful need, such driving pleasure. He did not know what gave him the strength to resist the deep surge of his own demand for release, again and again. He had reached some place in himself where the pain of resisting was transmuted into pleasure, and he thought, *This is madness,* and then, *the madness the poets speak of.*

He felt her sweat, smelled the perfume of her desire, and it, too, was pleasure and pain and madness to him. His mouth sought out her breasts under the light cotton covering, his tongue damping the fabric while his hand tried to reach them underneath, but the bodice of her dress was too tight.

With a cry of loss, Caroline felt him leave her, felt the air touch her suddenly exposed body with coolness. Drunkenly she reached for him. He caught her arm and drew her up onto her knees, and lifted the dress over her head. She was naked now, as they both knelt on the bed, and his hands ran hungrily down the length of her body, moulding breasts and waist and thighs as her head arched back and her skin shivered under the possessive seeking of his hands.

"Touch me, Caroline," he whispered, and of their own accord her hands flattened on his chest, and explored his shoulders, the powerful muscles of his hands, the tight firm stomach, his buttocks, his thighs...and then, with a moan of excitement, his virile, powerful sex.

Karim's breath hissed between his teeth, and she smiled and slipped her hands around the honeyed shaft, glorying in its strength, hungry with passion for him, and without conscious thought she bent and kissed it. When her lips touched it, she simultaneously heard the intake of his breath, and felt her own hunger. Her lips parted and she tasted him.

He pulled her up after only a few seconds. "Not this, not now, my beloved," he said.

He began to thrust into her again, his hands on her hips drawing her hard against him so that each thrust went to its depth, and the pleasure was so profound it was almost pain. She began to cry aloud with every thrust, and excitement mounted in her until mists shrouded her brain and she no longer knew where she was, or what she cried to him. Every stroke was too much, was not enough, was building to an explosion that she both feared and craved as he pushed his way in again and again past the million nerve ends of her being, sending sensation like fire roaring down her veins, across her skin, into her brain. She called, and begged, and cried to him, drunk with sensual delight and torment, until it suddenly exploded in her, spiralling out from somewhere deeper than herself to touch every greedy part of her. Then she sobbed, and moaned, and the blackness enveloped her in waves.

Now he felt his control slipping, and he bent over her again. She opened her pleasure-drunk eyes and smiled at him.

Then he held her head in his two hands and kissed her, deeply, tenderly, his tongue tracing the outline of those full, perfect lips, and it was this touch that was his undoing. Abruptly his body took its rhythm out of his control, and began to drive wildly, unconstrained, deep inside her, as if seeking the answer to some deep mystery in her.

Caroline's throat opened and, her head rolling from side to side on the pillow, she cried out her joy in the same rhythm that his body had set, so that her cries seemed to him to be his own, and her pleasure was his joy. It stormed through him, through them both, and for one instant he learned the answer that he sought. But even as he grasped it, it was carried away from him, for that answer always is cloaked in mystery.

Sixteen

"**G**ive the jewel back," said Thom Langley.

"Thom, I have already assured you several times that I do not have, and never have had, the Jewel Seal of Shakur. I'm not going to say it again."

"That's very wise. I'm told lies mount up in heaven, so you should limit the number of repetitions."

David Percy's jaw clenched. "You're being ridiculous, Thom. I understand your anxiety, naturally I feel it, too—"

"David, you've had one of the sheikh's minions working as your cleaner for the past six months! He couldn't take the thing because of your security, but he saw it, all right. I've seen a photograph he took of it. They've got other evidence, too, David, and this thing stinks!"

"What are you talking about, Thom?"

"You've had some hotshot investigative journalist on your tail for a couple of years now, David, and this time she's got you. I can tell you how you did it, if you've forgotten. You bribed one of the keepers of Prince Karim's treasury to take a plaster impression of the seal, and then you took that to a jeweller and got him to copy it in fake emerald, a stone that fools even experts. Then you gave the copy to the same keeper, and he smuggled it into the treasury and left it there, and smuggled the real one out."

Percy stiffened. "Where did you get this information?"

Thom Langley smiled. "It's going to be in the *Times* tomorrow. They called me for a quote. I said whether my daughter came back alive or not, she wasn't marrying a man like you if I had to take her hostage myself to prevent it."

The collector's eyes narrowed unpleasantly. "The *Times?*"

"You're starting to smell like a ratbag, David. What you need now is some damage limitation."

The room was bright, but the burning sunlight was filtered through the mass of greenery outside the windows, and as Caroline lay watching, a breeze caught the branches and played shadows upon the wall.

She was that tree, and Karim was the wind, and she was just as helpless to resist his power as the tree the wind. She could dance to it, but she could not resist. She lifted a lazy arm and cast graceful shadows of her own on the wall, humming a tuneless tune.

He would not hurt her. She understood it, believed it now. He had called her his beloved, and she had heard a note in his voice that she had never heard in any man's voice before.

She loved him, and she had to trust that love.

She was drained and revitalised all at the same time. When she stood up, her legs almost gave way underneath her, all the muscles weak with too much exercise. Caroline smiled involuntarily, remembering, an errant thrill chasing down her spine while her stomach and heart melted all over again.

She wrapped her robe around her and staggered limply into the bathroom. The bath pool was filled with hot water, and there was, for the first time, a woman attendant, whose obvious intention it was to wait on her. When Caroline tried to go under a shower, the woman smiled and waved her arms in a negative, drawing Caroline over to a long marble slab with a foam mattress on it. There by signs she encouraged her to lie down, and in a minute a bemused Caroline was being pummelled and massaged by powerful hands and arms, and an aromatic oil.

Half an hour later, feeling like the sultan's favourite, she was carefully ushered down the marble steps into the bath and given a bar of deliciously scented soap.

"Well, I could get used to this!" she told the woman, who smiled a broad approving smile and shouted an unintelligible response.

"Sheikh Karim?" Caroline asked, on a rising intonation. She lifted her hand from the warm water and gestured vaguely to ask if he had been here before. "Sheikh Karim was here?"

Laughing and nodding, the woman shouted "Sheikh!" and a few more words, accompanied by a sign language representation of a man in a hurry, who had showered and rushed out and was now busily dialling telephones and doing a lot of excitable talking and watching television.

Caroline was enjoying the game. She put on an exaggeratedly smiling face, then an exaggeratedly frowning one, but the woman shook her head and raised a finger for attention. Then she opened her eyes wide, raising her eyebrows and lifting both hands to indicate a man neither happy nor unhappy by what he heard, but very shocked and surprised.

At last, wrapped in a generous, thick white towel that

shrouded her from head to foot, Caroline made her way back into the bedroom to dress.

When she made her way into the main room, she found the situation just as the bath attendant had described it. There were three phones on the table now, and Rafi seemed to be manning all three at once. When he saw Caroline he lifted his mouth from the receiver and pointed.

"Watching TV," he said. "Grab yourself a drink, we'll be eating soon."

She went to the sideboard and poured some white wine into a glass, then made her way across the magnificent black and white marble floor and into the room where Karim, in a magnificent brocade robe and strange Oriental slippers, was sprawled on a divan, looking very much like a sultan at rest, watching the news channel.

He smiled up at her with a look that took her breath away and made her close her eyes in protest. He lifted his arm towards her, and when she approached took her wrist and kissed her hand, then her palm. "Are you well, Caroline?"

"Very well." She smiled lazily down at him, her eyes telling him all he needed to know.

"Sit here beside me," he commanded. "The story will be repeated shortly and I want to see if anything new has been added."

"A story to be published tomorrow in the *New York Times* will make the claim that the chain of evidence in the remarkable theft of the decade leads to David Percy, and says that the Great Jewel Seal of Shakur has been, and may still be, in his possession. The writer Camille Packer has been investigating crime in the antiques and art market for a book. She spoke to our correspondent."

Caroline sat forward and listened with fascination as Camille Packer announced that "fraud and dishonesty are rife in the antiques and art market all over the world" and then economically outlined the trail of evidence that pointed to David Percy. At the end of it, the interviewer said, "In your opinion, where is the Great Jewel Seal of Shakur now?"

And she said, "I think I've made it very clear where it went. There is no evidence to indicate that the Jewel has been moved or sold recently."

Next moment Caroline gasped to see her own parents on the screen. Her mother was weeping. They stood outside the house, in front of several mikes. Her father was reading from a piece of paper, looking into the camera at the end of every sentence. "We want to plead with Sheikh Karim for time," her father said. His eyes were damp and his voice unsteady. "It's a terrible thing that a jewel of such significance was stolen from him, but I urge him to remember that this family had no part in that theft. Caroline Langley, your hostage, is innocent of any wrongdoing. All she did was get engaged to the wrong man—" he looked bitterly into the cameras "—and I can assure His Highness that that engagement is now at an end as far as we are concerned. We urge David Percy to cooperate with the Barakati representative for the restoration of the sheikh's property and the safe return of our daughter."

He finished, and glanced down at her mother, who swallowed a few times, and then sobbed, "Please, David. Please, please. That's all I can say. Please don't let our daughter die for the sake of your art collection." Then she broke down completely.

They watched to the end of the item, and then he switched the set off. Caroline's eyes were wet. Karim turned her to face him and kissed away the tears on her cheeks. "Are you surprised?"

"A little," she said. "I've never seen my parents like that before."

"Perhaps it has taken a crisis to show them their own hearts."

She nodded.

"Karim, what will happen now?"

He shrugged. "David Percy has two choices, and only two. He can return the jewel, or he can go on in the lie that he does not have it. The second course would be very stupid and self-defeating, but men have been stupid and self-defeating before."

"What will you do?"

"We must wait and see." He kissed her again, tenderly, sweetly. "Caroline—"

But Rafi was at the door. "Nasir is on the phone."

They ran to the main room where the phones were, and Karim put the receiver to his ear. He spoke a few words in Arabic, then barked a startled question, while Caroline leapt from foot to foot in suspense.

At last he put down the phone and stared at Caroline and Rafi. "The Jewel Seal of Shakur was delivered to the door of the Consulate five minutes ago by an anonymous person. Nasir is on his way to the airport with it. The plane is fuelled and ready."

The next few hours were more of what the bath woman had mimed—telephone calls and television and bustle. The news that the jewel had been anonymously returned was released by the Consulate once the Royal Barakat jet was clear of American air space. The news channel reported that the palace in Barakat had still made no official comment.

David Percy, though he still denied all knowledge and denied having anything to do with the return of the jewel, was everyone's favourite villain.

By nine that night it was still only noon in New York and Caroline had telephoned her parents to say she was safe. Karim unplugged all the phones except one to which only

Nasir had the number and turned off the television. Rafi disappeared, leaving Caroline and Karim alone over dinner.

They sat among the cushions at the low table, as they had done before, and the food was even more delicious than it had been then. As before, Karim slipped delicacies between her lips, but it was the passionate look in his eyes that was nectar and ambrosia to her.

When they had eaten their fill, and the servant set the tiny coffee cups in front of them and withdrew, Karim lay back against the cushions and drew Caroline down against his shoulder. His hand stroked and played with her hair, watching in satisfaction how an obedient curl pressed around his finger and clung.

"Caroline," he began.

"Mmmm."

"Your father has said that you will not marry this man. Do you agree?"

She raised herself on an elbow and smiled at him. "Is it important to you?" she asked, knowing—*almost* sure of what his answer would be.

"Caroline, the jewel of my ancestor is returned, but I cannot return David Percy's jewel to him. Stay with me, Caroline."

Her heart floated free of her body and seemed to sail straight up to the light. "Karim," she breathed.

He misunderstood. He wrapped one strong hand around her upper arm and shook her a little. "You cannot marry this man, Caroline!"

"Is that an order, Your Highness?" she teased.

His jaw clenched, his nostrils flared, his eyes burned her. "Will you obey such an order from me?" he whispered.

"Oh, yes," she breathed.

"You will obey any order I now give you?"

She took a deep breath, but she had to trust her heart. She nodded.

"Then yes!" he said, nodding. "Yes, it is an order, my pearl past price. I order you to break your engagement and to stay here with me, to marry me and help me rule my people in good times and bad. Caroline, will you do this?"

Her heart was beating loud enough to deafen her. She opened her lips on a breathless gasp. "To marry you?" she whispered.

"Of course, marry!" he said roughly. He took her face in his strong hand and stared at her. "What did you imagine, Durri?"

"Well, correct me if I'm wrong, but this is the harem, and sheikhs do still have concubines," she smiled.

He turned her so that she lay on her back against the cushions, and he, beside and above her on one elbow, held her arm in his strong grasp and growled down at her.

"I do not want a concubine. I want you as my wife."

"Why?" she asked, knowing what his answer must be but needing to hear it.

"Caroline, because I love you as I will never love another woman." He closed the space between them and kissed her in rough impatience.

"But Karim, have you forgotten? Your wife—will you make me your queen?"

"Of course you will be my queen!" Her eyes widened in fear, and he said urgently, "You will be a fine queen for my people. They, too, will love you, and you will love them. Caroline, give me your answer."

"As it happens I already broke my engagement days ago."

It seemed to take a moment to sink in. "What?"

"I broke the engagement before you and I made love for the first time. That was why I had taken off my ring."

"You broke it? Why?"

"Because—because I was in love with Kaifar and I believed, in spite of his warnings, that he might—"

She broke off, smiling.

He stared at her, perhaps understanding the depth of her own love for the first time. "If Kaifar had asked you to be his wife, what would you have answered?"

Caroline was still smiling. "Kaifar never asked me."

Karim was not smiling. "He asks you now, Caroline. Do not torment me, but give me your answer!"

Her mouth lost its own smile as she looked into his hungry eyes. "Yes," she said simply.

He drowned her with his passionate kiss.

Later, he mused, "Is this why David Percy would not give up the jewel? Why did he not tell us at once that he was no longer engaged to you?"

"Because I guess he hasn't gotten my letter yet."

Karim frowned. "Letter?" he repeated, thinking of the two confiscated letters at present residing in his desk. He would mail them in the morning.

"I tried to phone, but all the international lines were down or something. It's a good thing, as it turned out, isn't it?"

"You were wearing his ring!"

She said, "I put on his ring the night I tried to escape because you had taken all my money and I thought it might pay for a taxi ride to the Embassy, Karim. And I kept it on after that as a protection from you."

His hand buried itself against her scalp. "You do not need protection from me," he told her, and then his mouth was hard and demanding on her own, melting her where she lay, making her hungry so that she wrapped her arms around his neck and pulled him down where he belonged, against her heart.

Epilogue

"**W**ell, Marta," said the anchorman, "I understand it looks like a safe ending to the hostage-taking incident in West Barakat."

"Yes, Barry, the—to give it its official name, the Great Jewel Seal of Shakur that was anonymously—I like that!—returned to the Consulate of the Barakat Emirates in Washington yesterday has been officially declared genuine and is now safely back in the Royal Treasury of Prince Karim. So far the hostage, Caroline Langley, the former fiancée of David Percy who was accused of having the jewel illegally, though, hasn't been released."

"I understand we're awaiting some kind of statement from the palace. Our correspondent is there. Andrea, what's the news?"

"I'm standing in front of the western door of the palace, where we've all been asked to wait. Rumour has it that Prince Karim himself—or since we're using the formal names this morning, Marta, that's—'' she consulted a piece of paper ''—Sayed Hajji Karim ibn Daud ibn Hassan al Quraishi—is planning to make a statement himself, but there's been no official confirmation. We're expecting him or a representative to say that the hostage will be released immediately, and perhaps she will even be turned over to embassy officials for the cameras later.''

Behind the reporter there was a shuffling and a murmuring, and Marta said, ''Andrea, looks like something's happening.''

The screen went empty as there was a cut to the camera focussed on the microphones standing at the top of the palace steps. Then to everyone's astonishment, the doors opened and Prince Karim stepped out, accompanied by a slender, smiling blond woman.

''My God!'' cried Marta involuntarily. ''Is that Caroline Langley?''

The couple strode towards the microphones, emerging from the shadows into the sunshine and pausing on the top step. A breeze caught the skirt of Caroline Langley's pale green dress and ruffled her curls lightly. She smiled bemusedly at the crowd of journalists shouting questions in the courtyard below.

Prince Karim stood in silence at the mikes, until the crowd fell silent.

He spoke first to his own people, telling them that the jewel was restored to the kingdom, and then that it was his great joy to tell them that the woman beside him would be his wife and their queen. He asked them to welcome her as they had welcomed his father's first wife, who, he reminded them, had also not been a Barakati, but who had been a wise influence on the nation and his father and an excellent queen to them.

Then, since most of his audience had not understood, he switched to English.

"First of all, I would like to thank all the people of the United States and also around the world for their patience during these past very difficult days. We have received messages of anger, but also many which expressed indignation not only at the wrong we did, but at the wrong done to us.

"The Jewel Seal of my ancestor Shakur is over 1,000 years old. There has never been any dispute over the ownership of this jewel. It is mine, as it was my father's before me, and back for many generations. As you have learned over the past few days, it is a significant symbol of stability to my people. I took drastic steps to reclaim it when it was stolen from me by thieves, and since there are other much admired jewels in my possession, it would be well for others of a like mind to these thieves to understand that I will always protect what is mine. By whatever method seems good to me."

Karim raised one autocratic hand, and out of the shadows behind him stepped Nasir, carrying a large, ornately decorated box. With a bow he offered it to this sovereign, who turned and raised the lid.

Then the prince clasped the Great Jewel Seal of Shakur in one strong hand, lifted it from its bed of silk and in a gesture not of triumph but of unmistakable authority held it up high over his head, where it glowed and glittered mesmerizingly in the bright sun.

"Let no one doubt that the Seal of my ancestors is my own!" he cried. The crowd, mostly of his own subjects, burst into wild cheering, while the television cameras zoomed in on the magnificent emerald held in that uncompromising fist.

He stood there, accepting his people's cheers and their

relief that all was well with the kingdom, his posture and attitude promising them that it would always be well under his rule. Then, with impeccable timing, he replaced the jewel in the box and solemnly closed the lid, and Nasir slipped back into the shadows, where armed guards were just visible.

Karim addressed the crowd again. The shouting died down.

"Now it is time for me to fulfill my part of the contract with the thief. However, I am here to tell you that I cannot return his own jewel to him. Caroline Langley will not permanently return to the United States."

Above the complete, breathless silence in the courtyard a bird suddenly sang. Then there was a huge indrawn breath as everyone breathed again at once.

"She will return there only to visit her family and prepare, and then she has promised to come back to Barakat and become my wife and the queen of my people."

The silence erupted into shrieks of amazement, babbled questions and breathlessly murmured commentary into a hundred microphones.

"Andrea, did you have any inkling of this?" Marta demanded.

"Not a rumour. Not a whisper," was all Andrea had time to murmur.

"Because this country has become such a focus of interest in these days, many of you now know that, many years ago, my father also took a foreign bride. That marriage lasted, through great joys and great sorrows, all his life. I am sure that my marriage with Caroline Langley will be a source of equal strength and happiness to both of us, and I am sure that it, too, will last all our lives.

"Like my father, I have vowed to my fiancée that she will always be my only wife. We will of course have a state wedding. I hope that many of you will come back to West Barakat again then. Thank you.''

Bedlam. They called, they cried, they shouted, they pleaded with Caroline to speak to them, to answer a few questions.

Karim turned to her, his eyes glinting with love. ''My pearl past price,'' he said, ''do you want to speak to them?''

Her heart was in her mouth with nerves. ''Will they pull the palace down if I don't?'' she joked. But she took strength from his smile and approached the microphones.

''Ms. Langley, is this a free choice you've made yourself?'' ''Ms. Langley, when will you be returning to the United States?'' ''Will you be under guard?'' ''Have you talked to David Percy, Ms. Langley?'' ''Did you break the engagement with him?'' ''Will you be seeing Mr. Percy when you return to the States?'' ''Caroline, why are you doing this?''

She took that one first, a smile teasing her lips. ''Because I love him,'' she said simply.

A thousand questions later, Prince Karim and his bride-to-be waved to the crowd and disappeared into the palace again.

''Well, Barry! I'm speechless!'' said Marta, who really was.

''You've missed your chance there, Marta,'' Barry said. ''But there are other eligible men in the family. Prince Omar has two motherless daughters now.''

Meanwhile, Karim and Caroline made their way to the Treasury. In Caroline's hands was the precious emerald in the box. She waited while Karim opened the doors and lifted the glass lid, and then she carefully set down the box, gently lifted the jewel out and replaced it in its case.

It caught the light, and she drew in an audible breath.

"So beautiful!" she exclaimed softly. "It really does have a magical glow, doesn't it? I almost believe it really *has* the power to ensure peace in the kingdom."

Karim nodded and securely locked the jewel's case.

"Now, beloved," he said. He smiled lazily, possessively down at his future bride. He unlocked another case and lifted the circlet of magnificent emerald flowers from the satin bed.

"It is the custom of kings in Barakat to give their brides a betrothal gift. I ask you again to accept this from me."

She smiled as he set the precious headpiece on her forehead, and turned her to admire herself in one of the mirrors adorning the walls.

"Karim, it's so beautiful," she breathed in astonishment.

But he could not let her look long. His head bent close. "You are more beautiful than any jewel, my pearl past price," he whispered, as his lips found hers.

*   *   *   *   *

Don't miss Omar's story,
THE SOLITARY SHEIKH,
book two in Alexandra Sellers's
highly sensual and exotic miniseries
SONS OF THE DESERT,
available in May 1999,
only from Silhouette Desire.

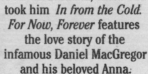

If you enjoyed what you just read,
then we've got an offer you can't resist!

Take 2 bestselling love stories FREE!

Plus get a FREE surprise gift!

Clip this page and mail it to Silhouette Reader Service™

IN U.S.A.
3010 Walden Ave.
P.O. Box 1867
Buffalo, N.Y. 14240-1867

IN CANADA
P.O. Box 609
Fort Erie, Ontario
L2A 5X3

YES! Please send me 2 free Silhouette Desire® novels and my free surprise gift. Then send me 6 brand-new novels every month, which I will receive months before they're available in stores. In the U.S.A., bill me at the bargain price of $3.12 plus 25¢ delivery per book and applicable sales tax, if any*. In Canada, bill me at the bargain price of $3.49 plus 25¢ delivery per book and applicable taxes**. That's the complete price and a savings of over 10% off the cover prices—what a great deal! I understand that accepting the 2 free books and gift places me under no obligation ever to buy any books. I can always return a shipment and cancel at any time. Even if I never buy another book from Silhouette, the 2 free books and gift are mine to keep forever. So why not take us up on our invitation. You'll be glad you did!

225 SEN CNFA
326 SEN CNFC

Name _____ (PLEASE PRINT)

Address _____ Apt.# _____

City _____ State/Prov. _____ Zip/Postal Code

* Terms and prices subject to change without notice. Sales tax applicable in N.Y.
** Canadian residents will be charged applicable provincial taxes and GST.
   All orders subject to approval. Offer limited to one per household.
   ® are registered trademarks of Harlequin Enterprises Limited.

DES99   ©1998 Harlequin Enterprises Limited

Coming in May 1999

BABY Fever

by
New York Times Bestselling Author

KASEY MICHAELS

When three sisters hear their biological
clocks ticking, they know it's
time for action.

But who will they get to father their babies?

**Find out how the road to motherhood
leads to love in this brand-new collection.**

Available at your favorite retail outlet.

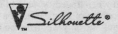

SILHOUETTE® *Desire®*

COMING NEXT MONTH

#1213 LOVE ME TRUE—Ann Major
Man of the Month
Why did international film star Joey Fassano ache with longing for a woman he couldn't forget? Heather Wade's parents had finally succeeded in transforming his lovely, free-spirited ex-girlfriend into a cool socialite. But now that Joey knew about Heather's little boy, even her powerful family couldn't keep him from seeing her again....

#1214 THE GROOM'S REVENGE—Susan Crosby
Fortune's Children: The Brides
He was out to destroy the Fortune name! Nothing was going to stop Gray McGuire from avenging his father's death, except maybe beautiful innocent Mollie Shaw. But was exacting his revenge worth the price of losing the love of his life?

#1215 THE COWBOY AND THE VIRGIN—Barbara McMahon
Well-bred Caitlin Delany had no business falling for sexy cowboy Zach Haller, especially since he was a one-night kind of man and she was a virgin! But the irresistible bachelor made her want to throw caution to the wind. And how could Caitlin say no to the man who could just be her Mr. Right?

#1216 HAVING HIS BABY—Beverly Barton
3 Babies for 3 Brothers
When Donna Fields returned from her trip out West, she brought home more than just memories. Nine months later, Jake Bishop was back in town and determined to make a family with Donna and their baby. If only he could convince sweet Donna that even a brooding loner could be a devoted dad—and a loving husband.

#1217 THE SOLITARY SHEIKH—Alexandra Sellers
Sons of the Desert
Prince Omar of Central Barakat was looking for a woman. To be precise, he was looking for someone to tutor his two young daughters. But one look at Jana Stewart and Omar was beginning to believe that *he* was the one in need of a lesson—in love.

#1218 THE BILLIONAIRE'S SECRET BABY—Carol Devine
He had vowed to always watch over his child, even if he had to do it from the shadows. And when tragedy struck, billionaire Jack Tarkenton knew it was time to take care of Meg Masterson and their child himself. Even if it meant marrying the only woman who had the power to bring him to his knees....